"Just what is a *gay book?*
—"A book attracted to books
of the same gender!"

Bob the Book
a novel by
David Pratt

Meet 'Bob the Book,' a gay book for sale in a Greenwich Village bookstore, where he falls in love with another book, Moishe. But an unlikely customer separates the young lovers. As Bob wends his way through used book bins, paper bags, knapsacks, and lecture halls, hoping to be reunited with Moishe, he meets a variety of characters, both book and human, including Angela, a widowed copy of Jane Austen's *Mansfield Park*, and two other separated lovers, Neil and Jerry, near victims of a book burning. Among their owners and readers are Alfred and Duane, whose on-again, off-again relationship unites and separates our book friends.

Will Bob find Moishe?
Will Jerry and Neil be reunited?
Will Alfred and Duane make it work?
Open
Bob the Book
to find all the answers…

"David Pratt takes a classic device from children's literature, the humanized object, and uses it not for a tugboat or lighthouse or velveteen rabbit but for a book on gay erotica. His voice is pitch-perfect as he follows his hero out into the world, creating a picaresque epic about books and bookstores, readers and collectors, conferences and bonfires. There's even a love story. *Bob the Book* is smart, funny, learned and, like the best bibliophiles, just a little crazy."
Christopher Bram, author of *Mapping the Territory* and *Father of Frankenstein*

"A bravura performance. David Pratt plays over the contemporary gay lit and psychology scene like Horowitz at a Steinway. His small gem of an idea goes way beyond allegory or even charm into a humorous yet serious look at what it is that men really want out of a relationship and what they are actually prepared to do to get it."
Felice Picano, author of *Art and Sex in Greenwich Village* and *Like People in History*

"You know how favorite books talk to your soul? Well *Bob the Book* is the story of what they say when you've left the room. This is a certifiable read-in-one-sitting book. And after you've talked it up, you'd rather buy another copy for that discerning friend then lend your own—parting with this book would be like turning off a necessary light."
Tom Cardamone, editor of *The Lost Library: Gay Fiction Rediscovered*

Bob the Book

Bob the Book

David Pratt

Chelsea Station Editions

New York

Cover and book design by Peach Boy Distillery & Design
Author photograph by Eva Mueller

Published as a trade paperback original by
Chelsea Station Editions,
362 West 36th Street, Suite 2R, New York, NY 10018
www.chelseastationeditions.com / info@chelseastationeditions.com

ISBN: 978-0-9844707-1-6
Library of Congress Control Number: 2010931818
First U.S. edition, 2010
Printed in the United States of America

For Ró, who makes all things possible

Bob the Book

Chapter 1
Bob the Book

Bob the Book felt mostly good about himself. He had not sold yet, but his comrade, Other Bob, another copy of the same book, had sold four months ago from the shelves of the Gay Diversions Bookstore on West Tenth Street in Greenwich Village, and Bob tried to wake each day feeling sure that his long shelf life meant he was uncommon and suitable only for the discerning. Bob's title (and the title of Other Bob) was *Private Pleasures: Myth and Representation in Male Photo Sets and Pornography from the Pre-Stonewall Era to 1979.* Bob had seven hundred eighty-five pages, an Introduction, Foreword, Preface, over two hundred black-and-white and color photographs, a deliciously detailed index in tiny type, thirty-six pages of citations, and on his cover, a sort of lumberjack with a drooping moustache, sideburns, stubble, and black chest hair curling out where his blue plaid flannel shirt lay open.

Bob had been written by Harrison R. Stone, Ph.D., a visiting professor at an Eastern University, who had spent thirteen years researching and writing Bob. Perhaps the subject matter was a little, well, indulgent? Some might even call it frivolous. But Bob truly felt Harrison Stone had found something important in all the "images" and "representations" he talked about, and Bob loved to think of each one of his crisp, eggshell pages, packed with type, the scholarly authority of those two hundred-plus photographs, and all the wisdom packed like DNA into the citations.

Bob sat on his shelf just above eye level, and from that vantage point liked to pretend he could choose from among the patrons that visited Gay Diversions the very one who would buy him. Occasionally a kindly-looking, salt-and-pepper schoolboyish type strolled through the door, filling Bob's bookish heart with hope, then draining it when the guy bought only a dusty tome from the discount bin and ding-a-linged quickly away.

But most of Gay Diversions' customers Bob rejected. The boy in cut-offs and white T-shirt, here for a copy of *Next* so he would know where to go clubbing or for a naked man calendar to take as a present to birthday revels in a Hudson Street loft. The boy had bulging arms and sweet nipples, but Bob decided he was not fit to buy him. Bob would not even look at that kind. Well, he might look, but they ignored him, and he, in turn, ignored them. *Fine.*

Fine. After the store closed up, in the dark, he watched the men in pairs or alone pass on the sidewalk, beyond the gate that came down over the door. He watched the neon pulsing and the taxi lights going by, and fell asleep listening to the muffled, pulsing music and hoots and hollers from Mr. Moose, the leather bar next door. He woke in the morning to the scrape of the gate being lifted. Maurice, the manager, unlocked and made coffee, and empty beer kegs clanged on the sidewalk as they were hoisted from the cellar of Mr. Moose and fresh, icy kegs vanished down, and a new day of hope without reason began.

Harrison Stone, Bob's author, lived nearby, in a brownstone on Jane Street. A sharp-featured man in a cardigan, he came to the store weekly, but he never looked at Bob. Stone had never looked at Other Bob, either. Instead, last time, Stone had purchased two different naked man calendars. Also, once a month, Stone made an appointment to meet with Maurice, who took him downstairs to make selections from his private collection of vintage male pornography. Stone rented more DVDs from the back of the store, from the section back behind the novels and art books and cultural studies (this last being Bob's category). *How common!* Bob thought. Wistfully, he reflected that even his own author could not pass muster as his ideal buyer: a man genuinely studious and thoughtful, well-groomed, with perhaps the suggestion of a "gym body." Or maybe a couple might want to take him home? What would it be like to be owned and read and discussed by two men in love? What, Bob wondered, would it be like to be in love himself? The wait for both a buyer and a true love could last long, Bob knew, but he told himself he did not mind. A buyer—just to think of it! *An owner and a reader!*

One night Bob woke from his bookish sleep, possessed by anxious thoughts. His close, high shelf held other, frightfully similar books, which his ideal buyer might buy instead: *The Semiotics of Skin: Muscle Men, Garage Boys and the Limitations of the Viewer Paradigm,* by Chase Alcott, Ph.D.; *Hieroglyphics of Desire: Representations of the Male Nude as Text in the Era Before Gay Liberation,* by Worcester Wetstone, Ph.D.—and many more. Titles trumpeted ideas explained in convoluted subtitles. A copy of Wetstone had sold two weeks ago. Now a thin layer of dust had collected on Bob. He consoled himself by noting that Lulu, the book next to him, whose title was *The Maverick Clitoris: Lesbian (In)visibility in Postwar American Culture, 1945-1964*, by Anne Marie Steinberg, had a slightly thicker layer of dust. Below, calendars of naked Marines and naked auto mechanics and naked Latino men and naked "freshmen" and naked "sophomores" sold out and had to be reordered and reordered and reordered. Maurice booked more appointments for Stone and other, mostly middle-aged and elderly men to visit the basement and choose vintage prints and slides and old eight-millimeter film transfers, and the shop rented more and more DVDs with titles like *Military Juice* (volumes 1-13), *Ebony Sharpshooters* (volumes 1-7), and other titles that punned endlessly on "tail," "come," "bare," "bear," and so forth.

The doorbell jingled. Harrison Stone was returning a stack of DVDs—black discs with white labels, boxed in clear plastic. Stone bought a paperback of *Greased Tails: An 18-Year-Old Dominican Auto Mechanic's Double Life as a Park Avenue Hustler.* And he bought a rainbow necklace.

"Traitor," Bob muttered.

"Do you mind?" hissed Lulu. "I was in a very restful space. I don't like the hostile vibration coming from you."

"But it's horrible!" Bob insisted. "Downstairs, one glossy photo goes for fifty bucks just 'cause the guy thinks he can't live without the boy in it. Then next week it's another fifty bucks for another photo of another boy he can't live without. Or sixty or sixty-five. Meanwhile, you go for $27.95, I go for thirty, if we go at all. It's outrageous! I don't understand why you don't see it!"

"I think you're making some very phalloeconomic assumptions," Lulu said. "I'm sorry, but this conversation feels toxic to me right now and I'm going to have to detach."

Bob picked up that Maurice had financial worries. He listened in on murmured phone conversations and heard the words, "sell the whole collection." Middle-aged men flowed in the front door like a rising river. They flowed down to the basement and poured back up, clutching flat, brown paper bags of photos. Someone bought Lulu. Bob felt relieved not to have her snapping at him, but it annoyed him when his new neighbor—Moishe, a new, young study of Orthodox Jewish gay men—fell against him with a thud. (Moishe's full title was *Beneath the Tallis: The Hidden Lives of Gay and Bisexual Orthodox Jewish Men*. His author was one Binyumin Stein, M.D.)

"Do you mind?" Bob said.

"*Nu*," Moishe sighed, "like I have a choice? We fall where we fall. They unload us, shelve us, push us here, push us there, you sell or you don't sell, they remainder us. *Oy*, if only someone would buy me!"

"Well, don't hold your breath," Bob said. He was surprised by a sympathetic, protective tone in his voice.

Meanwhile, Maurice became progressively disheveled and testy. His hair grew long and he paced the aisles. Harrison Stone now checked out as many as four DVDs in one evening, then returned them the next day and checked out four more, which to Bob did not compute, as just one disc advertised "over four hours of ebony action" or "five hours of pounding hard Marine muscle." Then Stone disappeared, for five weeks. When he returned he rerented many DVDs he had rented before, including *Taste My Sweaty Italian Ballsac IV* and *V*. Bob overheard him speaking to

Maurice, using such phrases as "not the one I needed" and "gives a better example of." Bob felt a chill along his binding. Stone and Maurice disappeared down the basement stairs. Twenty minutes later, at the cash register, Stone dropped more than a hundred dollars on three slides. As Maurice's assistant, Trip, made change, Stone held them up to the light coming in the front windows.

Now Bob stood awake every night. Beyond the gate booted or sneakered feet strode or ambled in the chilly night air. Sometimes an old man, bent and slow, stopped and slept just outside, like a used book no one would buy, Bob thought, and he felt strangely comforted. One night Bob swore the floor of the shop was sagging. He'd stood long months on his shelf, he knew his level and position well, and he felt certain that he now sat the tiniest bit lower. He tried to talk himself out of that feeling. Then, early one Saturday morning, he jolted awake with the sure knowledge that the floor had dropped a fraction of an inch. The basement had to be nearly empty of photos and slides now. Could there have been so many that they held up the main floor, that their sale would cause the boards to sag and the floor to...? Bob wished someone would hurry up and buy him. He lowered his standards a bit. Any genuinely interested party would do, so long as they had a clean place with some light. He hoped whoever bought him would read him through, but he realized this expectation might be too great. A cozy shelf would do fine. But what if a new owner resold him? The used-book bin at Gay Diversions was a sorry sight with its torn and faded jackets, and Bob had heard about used-book stores, jam-packed and windowless, horror stories about books fallen down behind radiators, left there for months on end.

He just wished for someone interested in keeping him.

Maurice was on the phone. "...and we have Harrison Stone's new book coming..."

Bob froze. Harrison Stone's *new book*? About what? A better, bigger, hotter topic? Stone himself had not come in the store for several weeks. Bob did not sleep that night. He tried to enjoy the morning light coming in the plate glass windows, but before he could settle into the warmth and think positive thoughts (for example, that interest in the new book might spur his own sale), the UPS van pulled up outside the store. Bob couldn't even think about how hot the UPS man looked in his brown shorts as Trip signed for the box.

Could it be? Maurice hovered about the box with a knife. When he cut the flaps open, there they were: two dozen copies of *A Mirror Crack'd: Affirmation and Denial in Gay Male Pornography from 1980 to the Present* by Harrison R. Stone, Ph.D. Foreword by Worcester Wetstone. Three hundred-plus photographs, most in color, and worst of all, to Bob's horror and disgust, a muscled male torso on the cover. Trip stacked the books in a pyramid at the front of the store, along with an announcement of a reading Stone would give. Four copies were also wedged onto the shelf next to Bob. Their names were Luke. They ignored Bob, who now felt ashamed of the campy retro muscleman on his own cover.

"Hi. You must be the old one," one of the Lukes finally said to Bob. "Oops, I mean one of the *originals*."

"Yes," Bob said evenly. "Welcome to my shelf."

"Whatever," Luke said, "it's not like we'll be around long."

Bob stole a glance at Luke's binding. Major New York publisher. Bob drew himself up and tried to feel a flush of pride in his university imprint.

"Quiet down!" said Moishe. "You're giving me *shpilkes*!"

Bob smiled at Moishe. He had begun to appreciate Moishe's pessimism. He had begun to like Moishe, now pressed right against him due to the wedging in of the Lukes. Just after noon, a thirtyish man on rollerblades pulled down one of the Lukes. "Later," Luke called out to Bob. Two other Lukes were bought the next day. A week later, Maurice was on the phone ordering more.

When Maurice got off the phone, a quiet, sweet-faced man about fifty stepped through the door. Bob had seen him often before. Today this man carried a plain brown shopping bag in his right hand. "Got rejects for you!" he called to Maurice with a chuckle. He hoisted the bag. "Glad to take 'em!" Maurice said. Bob had witnessed this ritual before: books returned, secondhand, to go in the discount bin in the back. He hoped that, if ever he were bought and then discarded, at least he could come back here, tacky though the discount bin looked, instead of getting lost in some horrible warehouse.

The man lifted books out of his paper bag. Trip stacked them behind the counter. "Now this one," the man said, and his hand went into the bag and took a book, but did not yet draw it out. "This one, you have to promise—" And he chuckled and drew the book gingerly out. It was the Other Bob, the other copy of Harrison Stone's *Private Pleasures*. "You have to promise me you won't tell Harrison. If he comes in and sees it, just promise—"

Maurice grinned. "Secret's safe with me!"

The man agreed that whatever he might collect on his secondhand books would be applied to a new purchase. He chose a paperback novel about a gay detective, and, at the last minute, a copy of Stone's new book. "This one has better pictures!" he joked to Maurice.

Bob tried to catch the Other Bob's eye as Trip carried him to the discount bin. Bob had seen Maurice scribble "$6—" inside Other Bob's front cover. Bob wondered if he might one day be resold for that amount. *Or less!* Bob tried to catch Other Bob's attention, but Other Bob simply lay in the bin, looking dazed and weary, looking, Bob thought, desperately as though he'd like to stand up straight, spine out, on a regular shelf, pressed between comrades. But instead he lay askew, disoriented, atop a coffee table book about two gay bodybuilders who considered themselves married and had taken each other's names. That book was called *A Perfect Love.* Now, Bob knew, those two men were, well, divorced.

"What is it?" Moishe asked.

"Look at the cover," Bob sighed. "Six dollars!"

"*Ach!*" said Moishe. "We should all live so long!"

Bob pressed against him just a little. Moishe pressed back. Bob pressed again and Moishe giggled. Bob tried not to think of the odds against the two of them ever being sold together.

That night Bob felt the floor sag again. This time others felt it, too, and a murmur ran along Bob's and Moishe's shelf. Other Bob said nothing. None of the discount books spoke. Two nights later, with a creak and a groan and a sudden slow monstrous splintering and the screams of hundreds of books, the entire first floor of Gay Diversions gave way, and all it had supported fell into the basement.

"Holy shit!" Maurice screamed the following morning when he came in. "Holy motherfucking fuck!" He stood stunned in the doorway and looked down into the jumble of books cascading into the pit of the empty basement. "Oh my God, oh my Christ!" he wailed. Of course he could not hear the cries of his books, many of which had been permanently injured and would now end up in the discount bin.

Maurice remained with his head in his hands for several minutes. Finally he raised it, gave two small sighs, and with the resignation that is the gateway between wild disbelief and mundane acceptance, he took up the phone, left a message for his insurance agent, and then surveyed the book-filled sinkhole that was his store. Bob, wedged awkwardly against Moishe, looked up. The pyramid of Lukes had fallen as well. Maurice reached down and pulled a Luke up. He dusted off the cover and set it in a corner of the front window, where the sun shone on it. He reached down for another. The sun did not yet shine on Bob and Moishe. Maurice picked up Luke after Luke. Trip arrived, pulled out his earbuds and said, "Oh, my God! Like, what happened?" For a few minutes Trip tried to steer the conversation toward the idea that this might mean he would have to take the day off, but Maurice was too distraught to pick up on it. Finally, opening time arrived. A trim and tanned fortyish man pushed his way in, wearing cargo shorts, a V-neck T-shirt, and sunglasses with a blue-silvery finish.

"Oh, my God!" the man said. "What in hell happened here?" He took off his sunglasses.

"I don't even know," Maurice sighed. "I just thank God no one was hurt."

The man put his sunglasses back on. "At least you have what I want!" he said crisply. He picked up a Luke from the small stack Maurice had reassembled in the window. "It's for a friend," he mused as Maurice rang up the sale. "Likes to think he's an intellectual, would die if anyone gave him a book of porn. So this is the perfect thing. And you know what else?" The man surveyed the fallen-in center of the store. "Do you have any of those, like, calendars called *Lads Who Lift Heavy Things*? While I'm at it I might as well purchase a little treat for *moi*."

"Such taste!" Moishe whispered.

"A clone!" Bob said, and grinned. "I thought they were extinct!"

"*Verwaspishe!*" Moishe returned.

Bob readjusted slightly, sliding down on top of Moishe. "Y'know, you're funny," he said.

"*Nu,*" Moishe said, himself readjusting, wriggling against Bob, "what took you so long?"

Sighing, Maurice continued slowly the rescue of his Lukes.

Chapter 2
Out into the World

Maurice took the money he'd made selling off his collection of vintage photographs, and he used it with the insurance money to fix his collapsed floor. Soon the floor had been repaired by two men in frayed jeans, big, dusty boots, and sleeveless T-shirts that revealed tans. Bob and Moishe were back on their customary shelf in Cultural Studies.

Fortunately, in the chaos, Maurice had neglected to reorder *The Maverick Clitoris: Lesbian (In)visibility in Postwar American Culture, 1945-1964*, so there was no new Lulu to keep Bob and Moishe apart. With no Lulu, the boys could enjoy long hours nestled up against each other, though Moishe had to fend off advances from Dirk, the volume on his other side, who was a copy of *Def Dick: Heterosexist Iconography of the Hip-Hop Nation*, by Orlando Salt. But Dirk lost interest, and Moishe pressed up against Bob and tried to crack him up with Yiddishisms. The two spent hours talking, joking about patrons and trying to guess what each would buy. It felt wonderful falling asleep next to Moishe, and knowing that he would be there where the sun came up and the gate was raised in the morning. But a book on gay Judaica and a book on retro erotica—bought together? It couldn't happen. Though with Moishe, Bob never worried about his subject matter or that it might be thought frivolous.

Moishe, too, spoke of his fear of losing Bob. Moishe was certain that a fan of *A Mirror Crack'd*, the new Stone book, would want to pick up Bob, too, especially as reviews of *A Mirror Crack'd* mentioned Bob quite favorably. Then, less than a week after reconstruction was finished, came a day Bob would always remember.

Around eleven in the morning the door jingled. A plump woman in her thirties with her black hair in a bun entered the store. Maurice chirped a hello, but already the woman was winding her way back to the Cultural Studies shelf. Her index finger ran along the spines: P, Q, R, S. The moment she spotted Moishe she said, "Ah-ha," pulled him down, turned, and as Bob cried out to his departing friend.

"I'll... I'll look for you!" Bob stammered helplessly. Moishe called something in reply that he could not make out. The woman strode to the cash register, pulled out an American Express card, and soon Bob had lost forever the only other book he had ever really loved.

Bob cried all that night. Other Bob lay silent in the discount bin. In the morning, the hot UPS guy in brown shorts brought a box that contained a new copy of *Maverick Clitoris*. This Lulu was a separatist, who resented that lesbian and gay male cultural studies were shelved together at Gay Diversions. Meanwhile, on his other side, Bob had the pain and boredom of putting up with four Lukes. The Lukes had subtle ways of reminding Bob that they sold faster than he did. They referred to him as Harrison Stone's "old book," and they talked about little other than their hot photographs, taken from '80s and '90s porn. That a scholar like Worcester Wetstone had penned their Foreword did not impress them; they were more interested in cruising boys who came in wearing running shorts to purchase naked-men calendars or CDs of dance music. "Ooh! I hope that one buys me!" they said, or, "Oh, honey, he could read me in bed anytime!" They were proud of the soft-focus nude male torso flexing on their covers. Bob missed Moishe terribly.

Moishe had been quiet and droll. He was, by his own admission, "pessimistic as only a Jew can be, optimistic as only a Jew can be." Bob loved that. Moishe had felt reverently toward his own subject matter; he was proud to do the service of spreading the word on an important and neglected topic. He had hoped to be purchased by someone doing scholarly work about Judaism or sexuality, but he was shy about mentioning his dream to Bob. They both knew the likelihood was slim that one person would purchase them both. Now Moishe was gone. Bob hoped that dark-haired woman was a scholar, as Moishe had wished for. Moishe had mentioned his wish to be marked up, highlighted and underlined, with Post-its stuck to his pages, and to live with someone forever. Bob hoped that Moishe's dream was now coming true.

Bob fantasized that one day he himself would be purchased by a scholar, that that scholar would bring him to a lecture by the dark-haired woman and she would have Moishe in tow, that they would come close enough to call out to one another. Perhaps Bob's owner would come speak to Moishe's owner at the end of her speech. But Bob had little time for such speculation. A few days later, in early fall, a frowning man in his late thirties bought him. He flipped through Bob as he walked down Hudson Street under a perfect blue sky. That evening, at home, the man, whose name was Peter, curled up with Bob in an overstuffed chair by a window facing the rustling trees sheltering the sidewalks of Perry Street. The man seemed intent on reading Bob, perhaps all the way through, which Bob had always dreamed of. Bob had heard the old saws about scholarly studies: "They'll admire you, they'll never love you," or, "They'll only come to you when they want something." Peter even did some underlining and stuck a Post-it note on one of Bob's pages, all of which made Bob feel good and close to Moishe, wherever he might be.

When Peter finished his reading he set Bob aside with a Gay Diversions bookmark stuck in at page forty-seven, and went to brush his teeth. Bob now found himself in a difficult position.

From the floor by Peter's overstuffed chair, Bob could see classics of gay literature up on Peter's shelves, in hardcovers and paperbacks: *Dancer from the Dance, The Best Little Boy in the World, A Boy's Own Story, Surprising Myself.* Bob longed to join them, to talk to them and hear their stories. But he was stuck on the floor by Peter's chair with a jumble of reading material Peter did not necessarily love but just meant to get around to. There was Gina, a copy of *The New Yorker*, who picked fights with Tad, a copy of the *Vanity Fair* Hollywood issue. Tad provoked Gina by discussing the number and the content of his ad pages. He called Annie Leibovitz "Annie" and said, on very slight pretext, "Oh, yes, Bruce did a great photo of Jake Gyllenhaal for me."

"*'Bruce'* didn't do anything for you," Gina snapped, angry that no one recognized the names of her *New Yorker* writers. ("Malcolm Gladwell?" she said. "Roger Angell? Hello? Like, where have you people been?" "L.A.," Tad said matter-of-factly.) "Get a grip!" Gina added. "You were cranked out of a printing plant in Sandusky, like the rest of us. You just have *pictures* from Hollywood! *'Bruce'* doesn't even know you exist!"

While Gina and Tad bickered, Clarice, a copy of Sylvia Plath's collected poems, moaned to everyone within listening range, "God, I can't take this! I willingly embrace death!"

"Not fast enough for me," said Hank, a paperback copy of *Armored Cav: A Guided Tour of an Armored Cavalry Regiment* by Tom Clancy. "Man, I think you're all a bunch of nutballs!" Hank had been lent to Peter by his brother, who'd insisted he'd like it. Peter had not read Hank and had no intention of reading him, and Hank knew it and so did everyone else. ("Guns," Tad deadpanned. "How fascinating.") This made Hank insecure and angry, as, of course, did the presence of so many gay books. So Hank turned his guns, such as they were, on those around him. "Y'know what I say about magazines," he grinned at Gina. "Here today, gone tomorrow!" And to Bob he said, "*'University press?'* Is that like some kind of little work project for scholarship kids?" Hank liked to boast about his detailed descriptions of the M1A2 Main Battle Tank, and the AH-64A Apache Attack Helicopter. He pointed to his reviews ("I got a beaut from the Miami *Herald!*") until Gina said, "Well, they were talking about the hardcover edition weren't they? And your cover is soft."

"I'll show ya the difference between hard and soft!" Hank shot back. "I was thinkin' we could have a little fun, Sweetheart, before you get recycled!"

"Is that what you were *thinkin'*?" Gina replied. "Well you can go right on *thinkin'* it, but I don't believe we're gonna be *doin'* it!"

"Christ, this is intolerable!" moaned Clarice, to which Tad answered, "Would the Dead Poets' Society please keep a lid on it!"

Then Nigel entered the fray. Nigel was a copy of *Winnie-the-Pooh* that Peter had brought down for his niece when she stayed over the weekend before. "I say," Nigel complained, "I'm ever so cross with all of you!"

"Ooh!" said Tad. "A book about a bear! Which reminds me, Gina, have you seen my picture of Bob Hoskins? Annie took it. *Tiddley-pom!*"

Bob the Book was miserable. He lay quietly on Peter's floor, and did not point out to the others that he was the only one Peter was actually reading. He thought of Moishe, hoping he was being read and underlined as he had always dreamed, and that he might get to visit important conferences or classes.

Three days later, Peter took Bob with him to an all-natural café near his apartment. Peter sipped a frozen fair-trade cappuccino drink and stared out the window at traffic. Bob believed Peter was lonely, and he thought he saw him eyeing good-looking men who passed. This reminded Bob of Moishe. He looked away. Then his heart stopped. There, on the table next to him, was a copy of *Beneath the Tallis: The Hidden Lives of Gay and Bisexual Orthodox Jewish Men* by Binyumin Stein, M.D.

"Moishe!" Bob hissed.

"No," said the book. "Hal."

"Aren't all copies named Moishe?" Bob asked.

"*Putz!* Do I look like all copies?" Hal replied. "I'm a privately printed edition. From back when Stein couldn't get a publisher.

Then we become a success, Stein goes on a tour, doesn't call his mother for three days—you know she's legally blind and a widow? Anyway, a big publisher takes him on, and those are the Moishes. You were obviously shelved near one of them," Hal said, peering at Stone's name on Bob's cover. "Me, I was sold out of the back of a station wagon. A Chevy. Needed new shocks, my binding almost came loose, but so what, I'm not complaining, I survived. Are you looking for any special Moishe?"

"Yes!" Bob answered. He described his Moishe to Hal, detailing Moishe's dreams, as Moishe's appearance would be more or less the same as all the other Moishes.

"Yeah, yeah," Hal said. "Y'know, I think I know him. Right when the Moishes came out us Hals got mixed in with them at this psychology conference. I think I met your boy on a display table, really sweet, nice. He was unsold, though, at the end of the conference, and so he probably got shipped to your store. I was sold at the conference. Stein was trying to unload us Hals first. His mother's basement was full of us. Can you imagine? Forty-five and a doctor and he still lived with…"

Bob interrupted and described to Hal the woman who had bought Moishe.

"*Oy vay ist mir.* I wouldn't know," Hal said. "This guy here who's reading me—Isaac? Not a scholarly type. He's just reading me for personal reasons. He's not about to go to some big conference on the subject."

Just then the man named Isaac reached for Hal. As he plopped Hal into a worn black briefcase, Hal called out, "If I find your Moishe, who should I say—?"

"Bob!" Bob cried out. "Good luck!" He called out Peter's name and address, but wondered if Hal had heard it, or if it would do any good. Peter rose a few minutes later, took Bob in hand, and sauntered back to his apartment.

The situation at home had not improved. "Take a look at my cover," Tad cooed to Hank. "It says that I'm 'Our Biggest Issue Ever!'"

"Look, dude," said Hank, "I told you: that's not my thing!"

Peter soon finished Bob and placed him up on a shelf, far from the warring magazines, though Bob found the volumes on his particular shelf less than interesting.

As weeks passed, Bob noticed Peter working many more hours at his computer. Then he took long afternoon naps. Some days he woke coughing and popped pills from a cylindrical orange plastic container. Peter often had a friend over—Sheila, a woman with long brown hair and many rings. Bob began to think Sheila was not a regular friend. She came the same time each week, usually for about three hours, and Peter always had a list of chores ready for her to help him with.

One morning the two of them sat at Peter's dining table and went over some insurance forms. Bob felt fear creeping up his binding. Peter talked to Sheila about medications he was taking that the insurance did not cover. Then Bob heard Peter say the words "sell some things." Sheila said, "Oh, Peter, I hope not! There must be something we can do!" But Peter rose, went to his bookshelves, and ran his finger tips along the spines of his books! Bob shuddered when Peter's finger reached his spine. Bob saw how much Peter loved his books, and how it hurt him even to think about selling them. He turned to Sheila. "I suppose some of them could go," he said. "I could make a few hundred."

Sheila looked on sympathetically from her seat at the dining table. "If you really must," she told Peter, "then the place to go is the book sale at the Armory."

"Sounds like something for collectors," Peter said. "I don't have anything leatherbound."

"They have bins and bins of regular paperbacks, hardcovers, anything and everything," Sheila said. "They dump 'em all together, and they pay reasonably well. I can help you pack some boxes. I have a friend in the Slope with a van."

Peter took several seconds to answer. "Let me think about it," he said.

That afternoon Bob listened to Peter, coughing throughout his nap. In the end Peter got up and phoned Sheila and said he would take at least one box of books to the Armory. They could do it on the subway. He said he knew this wouldn't mean much money, but he had to do something, and one boxful was all he could bring himself to sell.

To Bob's dismay, Peter packed him in that one box. Bob wondered, had he not been good enough? Peter had finished him. Was his topic not important? Had Harrison Stone not written well enough? Peter wedged Bob next to a book called *Making the Most of the Life You Want*. Her name was Sunny, and she had a blurb on her cover from Oprah Winfrey. When Bob confided his fears to Sunny, she said, "I don't think of it as being discarded. I think of it as entering a new phase. It's not about me as a book."

"But who'll buy us? Where will we end up?" Bob fretted.

"If you take care of the now," said Sunny, "the future takes care of itself. My chapter nine starts out with a quote from Susan Sarandon, who says..."

But Bob wasn't listening. He looked wistfully back at the gay classics Peter was keeping, and asked himself, *Why couldn't I have been written by Edmund White? Why couldn't I have been some classic that everyone's heard of?*

Meanwhile, Sunny counseled a dejected book on gay dating that lay next to her. "You are not your content," she told him. "Maybe Peter just wasn't ready for you." Peter shut the flaps of the box.

The subway car smelled and the lights flickered. Peter and Sheila sat silently. Peter shifted the box to let fellow passengers get on or off. Inside, Peter's books complained and worried.

"Experience is neutral!" Sunny insisted. "It's what you make of it!"

Bob felt a little better when flecks of sunlight filtered in during the walk from the subway to the Armory. At the Armory the box was received by a sweet-voiced volunteer in a close room near the entrance. "Just put it there," she trilled, with a wave of her hand. A man in a blue denim shirt, sleeves rolled up to reveal plump, hairy arms, pulled the box flaps apart, and scanned the spines of Peter's books. His face became stiff as he discovered Bob and some of the other gay books. He beckoned to another volunteer, then punched some numbers into a calculator and paid Peter in cash what he had determined the books were worth.

Next, the man scribbled prices in each book. Bob would go for ten dollars. (Bob thought the man scribbled a little aggressively, digging his pencil into the page.) Sunny was priced at one dollar. "Money," she proclaimed, "has nothing to do with value." But to Bob she sounded tense. Bob understood why the Other Bob had lain so dispiritedly in the discount bin at Gay Diversions. The life of a used book was humiliating: first, the knowledge that Peter didn't want him, then being jammed into the box, the trip on the subway, the look from the man in the denim shirt, the harsh digging of the pencil.

Now Bob, along with dozens of other books, was stacked on a pallet. Through a wide door at the other end of the room came a forklift truck. Sunny was in the stack next to Bob. "My goodness!" she said, trying to keep her voice even as the forklift drew near, louder and louder. "My, my. Every day's a new adventure..." Bob looked around. Peter and Sheila were gone.

The forklift took its load bumpily through the hallways of the Armory. The ride excited Bob. He hadn't taken this sort of a ride since the UPS truck had brought him to Gay Diversions. The forklift turned a corner. There before him was the Armory, vast, high, and dim. People pored over thousands of books—table after table. Bob could hear, mingled with the chatter of people, the moans and cries of books dumped in a jumble, books that missed their owners, books that feared for their fates, that had heard rumors that leftovers would be taken away and shredded. The forklift slowly rolled into the fray.

"My word!" Sunny said softly, looking around. Her voice caught as she said "My dear, dear, sweet Lord!"

Bob pressed himself to her and remembered pressing himself against Moishe. *This is it*, Bob decided. As tables of books passed, as the people jostled and wove, he told himself, *I'll just ask every book I see. I'll—well—I can't make anyone buy me, but somehow I'll find him. Somehow in all this I will find him and I will be near him and they will not ever take me away from him again!*

"Shit!" Sunny mumbled.

Chapter 3
Three Musketeers

Bob and his comrades cascaded over a broad folding table set up in the middle of the Armory. Human hands reached for them, straightening them into stacks. Rarer, more exquisitely bound books stood at the other end of the cavernous space, classified by genre or author. Obscure books and paperbacks, like Bob and company, priced at one or five or ten dollars, lay in crooked piles, scanned by people already exhausted, whose eyes searched sometimes for a special title, other times for any cover that caught their eye.

As Bob fell, binding first, onto the table, a female voice protested, "Ouch! I say!"

"I'm sorry!" Bob called.

"Well, not your fault, what?" said the voice in an impatient British accent. On the other side of him, Bob could hear Sunny gamely telling another book, "Look, everything is temporary."

Bob looked at the book that had said "Ouch:" a handsome

paperback of Jane Austen's *Mansfield Park*. Bob liked the look of her and found encouragement in her crisp tone, so he introduced himself to her.

"Pleased to meet you," she said. "My name is Angela. Not a lot of room here, what?"

"I don't know what we can do," Bob said. "Hope for the best, I guess."

"Always," said Angela. "You and I are fortunate."

"How so?" Bob asked. He had never before thought of himself as fortunate, except when he and Moishe were together.

"Austen's a perennial seller," Angela said, "and you're a scholarly book. No idiot's going to buy you, or read you and throw you out the next day."

"But I ended up here," Bob sighed. He thought Angela was just being nice to him. On the other hand, why did people always put "just" before "being nice?" Being nice was not insignificant. "I never thought Peter, my owner, would sell me, but he needed money."

"Vagaries of fortune," said Angela. "Can't do a thing about it! I've been read four times, twice by the same person. I hope I'll be read again, but if not, as you say here in the Colonies, 'them's the breaks.'"

"I suppose," Bob said, casting a nervous eye around. People loomed over him, scanning covers. A middle-aged man with a dark tan and a hairy face riffled through him but put him back. Sunny was trying to lift the spirits of some other paperbacks to Bob's left. "You are not your cover," she said. "There's a quote from Gandhi, in my second chapter, and he says—"

Light fell through the pebbled glass in the Armory roof, diffused and dimmed by the time it reached the books. Afternoon was ending. The crowd thinned. Angela had been picked up, checked for a price, then put back closer to Bob. They began to converse about the kinds of readers they liked. Bob had not mentioned Moishe yet, and his dream of being underlined and highlighted. He didn't know what other books might be around. Maybe another one like Hank, the armored cavalry book. You had to watch and wait before you spoke.

Sunny broke into the conversation between Bob and Angela. "I, for one, like being the kind of book that someone comes back to again and again. Read a little here or there, take away a little nugget of wisdom for a friend..." She looked first at Bob, then at Angela. "I'm sure the two of you are the same way. *Oops!*"

For a man's large hand had picked Sunny up. He called out, "Tina!" and he waved Sunny over his head. A woman's voice from several yards away answered, "What?"

"Come here, you've gotta see this!"

The woman named Tina loomed. The man held Sunny out to her. In an exaggerated voice he said, "Tina, I just thought I should *share* this with you!"

"Oh, my God!" Tina said. "Can you believe it?"

"This is the book Julie swore by, right?"

"Yeah, when she was in her 'create your own reality' phase, or whatever. In other words, when she was unemployed!" Tina took Sunny and turned her over. "Oh my God, this is too funny! Who can we get this for as a joke? How about Tom? He hates this kind of crap!" Tina opened Sunny. "Listen to this: 'You can optimize a whole meeting, or your morning cup of coffee. Not a moment of life should pass on which you do not practice optimization.'"

The man took Sunny back. "I think that I'm going to optimize my life right now and not buy this book!" He threw Sunny onto the table with a plop.

"No, wait!" Tina said, picking up Sunny. "It would be such a great gag gift if we could think of the right person."

"Tina," the man said, "let's just get out of here. They're closing up."

"You're right," Tina said. "Let's go optimize a latté!"

Tina tossed Sunny back and the two of them walked away.

Sunny lay askew, partially open where Tina had left off reading her. She didn't say anything. She didn't even cry. Now Bob truly understood the despondency of the books in the secondhand bin at Gay Diversions. Finally a faded, broken-backed romance novel on the other side of the bin said softly, "Welcome to reality, honey. When they say used, they mean used." Angela, in a clipped voice tinged with anger, added, "Could have been any one of us. Any one. There are people who don't like Austen."

The Armory began to clear out. The books had picked up the information that the sale would continue the next day, maybe longer. Bob and his friends felt relieved, all except Sunny, who'd stayed quiet since Tina's boyfriend had tossed her back. Bob now missed Sunny's pep talks.

After the staff turned out the lights and locked the Armory for the night, Bob and Angela resumed their conversation. His voice low, Bob began to tell Angela about Moishe—what a fine book he was and what he had dreamed. "Lovely!" Angela exclaimed. "Simply lovely. I congratulate you on your love!"

"But I'll probably never see him again," Bob said. He told Angela about the coffee shop encounter with Hal.

"But perhaps you will see him," Angela said. "And if not, you have a very beautiful memory, which is all we can hope for, isn't it? To have that memory to go to every now and then? I have such a memory, for I was once in love. His name was Reggie. He was a copy of *Tristram Shandy* and simply marvelous. Funny and kind. Oh, he could keep me entertained for hours. I loved him very much, but I lost him. Water damage in the apartment, you know. Our owner had taken Reggie down. He was lying on the floor and he drowned. I was up on the shelf and was spared. Until the man moved and sold me, and I ended up here. Vagaries of fortune, you see? One of our friends was a marvelous volume of Boethius. I think he was kept. But you learn to let Fortune's wheel turn, Bob, and you try to remember the good times."

Now Bob became aware of a muffled sobbing close by.

"Hello?" Angela said.

"Who's there?" said Bob. It wasn't Sunny. Bob stared hard into darkness and made out a small, nice-looking paperback called *A Pocket Book of Gay Love Poems.*

"What's the matter?" Bob asked.

When the small volume finally collected himself he managed to stammer out, in a trembling voice, "I was in love, too. Once."

"Oh?" said Angela. "Tell us."

"He was my life" the small book said. "But—"

"But what?" said Bob.

"He was... *He was burned!*" The book burst out crying again. Angela and Bob simply let him cry a while before they asked any more questions.

"It was in Alabama," explained the small book, who then stopped to introduce himself as Neil. "Just a tiny gay and lesbian bookstore, very discreet. We thought something was wrong though, the way these serious-faced people marched in one day and started buying so many of us. It turned out they came from a church nearby. That Saturday night they were having a book burning: gay books, lesbian books, anything dangerous. Or liberal. *Catcher in the Rye.* Chaucer, for Heaven's sake! It was awful. The screams... I can't even think about it. But I was saved. It turned out they didn't have a permit, so they had to put out the fire and the bookstore owner managed to get some of us back. I was in shock. We'd been in full view of the fire. I saw Jerry go, Jerry was my... And I saw him go and he called out to me and said he loved me, and then he was gone. Eventually the store went out of business and someone from up here bought us. Someone running a sale like this one. I've had a couple of owners since then. And now I don't know what to do."

"Well," a deep voice said suddenly from the darkness, "if you ask me, this Jerry got what he had coming to him!"

They all froze.

"Who's there?" Bob and Angela said at once. They looked up, and in the dim moonlight filtering down from the ceiling they saw a hardcover looming over them: *How to Live: Restoring Christian Values to a Secularized Society,* by The Reverend J. Terrence Carmody.

"Name's Fred," said the Carmody book. "I overheard every word you said." He sneered at Neil. "And you disgust me! You're what's wrong with this society. And you!" he glowered at Bob, "from some fancy 'university press,' a seven hundred-page excuse for pornography. Disgusting. And who's your friend? Some so-called foreign 'classic.' People playing croquet on rich estates. You know there's only one book people need, and that's the Holy Bible!"

"If that's the case," Angela shot back, "then they don't need you!"

But Fred went right on, condemning all three of the friends, and adding that Tina's boyfriend had been right to throw Sunny back. "Self-help!" Fred sneered. "The only true help comes from Our Lord!" Bob shuddered to think what this book would say if Moishe were here. Hal might face Fred down, but sweet Moishe would have no more idea what to say than Bob had. Or Neil.

Then a new voice rang out.

"Fy on ye!" it cried in Fred's direction. "Ye ar naught worth!" Then to Angela, Bob, and Neil it said warmly, "Ye shuld nat have ado with none of hys felyship!"

The three books looked up. "My goodness!" Angela murmured in admiration. Over them stood a book with an orange cover, from which Bob could read the words, Malory, *Complete Works*.

"Ye ded a fowle shame!" the orange-covered book thundered at Fred.

"What in Jesus' name?" Fred said. "You some kinda foreign interventionist?"

"I woll nevir meddill with you!" the orange cover returned. "But woll deffende such goodlye felowes as thys be!"—and he indicated Angela, Bob, and Neil.

Fred refused to argue with any "Communist foreigner," and so, after hurling a few last words of condemnation, withdrew from the conversation.

"Fy! Fy!" the orange cover shouted at him.

Bob whispered to Angela, "I wish that couple from before had found Fred and made fun of him, instead of Sunny."

Angela looked up at Fred and full voice she said, "No use wishing. That kind never learns. We just don't bother with them."

Fred looked as though he wanted to say something more, but the orange cover was glowering at him, so he didn't.

After a few moments awkward silence, Neil spoke up. "You know what I wish?" he said.

"What?" asked Bob.

"I wish the three of us somehow, y'know, could stay together. Like, if one person bought all of us."

"Well, that's never going to happen!" Bob said.

"Oh?" said Angela. "And why not, pray?"

"One person?" said Bob, "Who happens to pick out a study of gay photographs, a book of love poems, and a copy of Jane Austen? Sure!"

"I think it can be managed," Angela said lightly.

Bob stopped. He had already learned that Anglea meant what she said. "How?" he asked, still not daring to believe.

"I can speak to someone," Angela said.

"Speak to someone?" Bob repeated.

"Who?" asked Neil.

"How shall I put it?" said Angela. "Us Austen books, like a lot of fiction, sometimes have the ability to communicate with people, and people even communicate back to us, silently."

"I've never heard of this," Bob marveled.

"Of course not," said Angela. "It's your first time being resold."

"I don't understand," Neil said.

"Not many new books learn how to speak to readers," Angela explained. "You're new, all crisp and perfect and great reviews and a place near the front of the store—or in my case, the back, but classic. I was by Jane Austen, for Heaven's sake. Of course someone would buy me! But then you're bought and read, maybe discarded, and you begin to learn how things are. Your binding's cracked, your pages dog-eared, so you have to learn how really to communicate, reveal to people who and what you truly are." Bob looked more closely and saw that, indeed, Angela's spine was cracked. Funny, she was so spirited and kind that he had not noticed the damage before. "You learn how to spot book lovers and speak to their souls," she continued. "Make them want you for more than the painting on the cover, or for the idea of owning a 'great book.' And what you'll find is that certain people—true book lovers—are more susceptible to your communications than others. And that susceptible kind is the kind who's going to be all over this place. We simply have to spot such a person, a gay chap, obviously, and I think we can plant the idea in his head to buy us three musketeers all together."

Bob volunteered that, due to the notoriety of the new book written by his author, some gay man just might be susceptible.

Neil piped up. "And I'm one of those 'wouldn't it make a nice gift?' books. I wasn't damaged too badly. I'm the kind of thing someone would grab for a buck just to have around."

Bob agreed, but this made him think of Sunny, almost sold as a gag gift. She'd still not spoken a word.

"I would say we make a good trio," said Angela. "If I can just speak to someone. Some literature lover who remembers paperback classics from college, who remembers the first time he bought a Fielding or a Thackeray or a Dickens all on his own. An English major type who read summers, but who also has, you know, a sense of fun about *la vie gai*, what? No one's all one thing. People are surprises. I think I can come up with someone."

Bob the Book went to sleep that night feeling happier and more optimistic. If Angela could pull this off, maybe the three of them could stay together and someday even find Moishe. Beside him he heard Angela's gentle breathing and murmuring in her sleep. He wondered if she dreamt of the book she had loved that had drowned. Behind Bob, Neil was awake, nervous. Bob stole a look up at Fred, silent now, but still tall and threatening. They slept in his shadow. But Bob could also see the orange cover, shining dully in what little moonlight came in. He would protect them. At the same time, around all these classics, Bob felt his subject matter made him less important than some other books. Yet Angela seemed to have no problem. And Neil had to understand, and Sunny, well, if she ever recovered, Sunny seemed to accept everyone. She kind of had to.

Bob felt excited and anxious over this hope Angela had raised that she, Neil, and Bob could stay together. She sounded so sure of herself. And yet "communicating" with people? He thought he might have heard murmurs of such a thing back at Gay Diversions.

He looked around and noticed a book with a white cover and spine, resting close by. "Hey!" Bob said cheerfully. "I guess you can't sleep, either."

"Do I sleep?" the book asked. "I don't think I do. I don't think I think. Or are they thinking for me? Perhaps they are. Are they here? I do not know."

"Excuse me?" said Bob.

"Perhaps they are close and it is their voice I hear. Perhaps they are far away. Wouldn't that be a good joke? I must go on."

"What's your name?" Bob asked, for he could think of nothing else to say.

"Do I have a name? I think I do," said the book. "Or I did have a name, at one time, at a time I cannot remember, I did have a name."

Bob had no idea how to proceed with this book. He stared into the darkness that covered the book's spine, until he made out the words: *Beckett: Molloy, Malone Dies, The Unnameable.* Bob looked around. He thought there might be a copy of *Waiting for Godot*, too. But of course there wasn't.

Chapter 4
Getting Picked Up

The next morning, volunteers came early to open the Armory. Lights flickered on and shuffling feet could be heard. "Good morning!" Angela called, as Bob blinked himself awake. "Good morning," Bob and Neil answered softly. Bob could tell from Neil's voice that he had not slept. Bob stole a glance up at Fred, dark and motionless, probably still asleep. Bob silently reprimanded himself for worrying what Fred might be doing or thinking, or if he was watching. Close by, the orange-covered book looked to be sleeping, too. On his front Bob now saw a picture of two knights on horseback, their lances aloft.

Bob hoped Angela would say more about how she planned to get herself, Bob, and Neil all sold together. None of the books knew for certain how long the sale would continue, or what might become of unsold books when it ended. Rumors circulated, one contradicting the next: "We'll be shredded!" "We'll be donated, somewhere nice!" "Baloney! That donation stuff is for kids' books. No one throws kids books out; they got it made. We'll probably get burned!"

"Oh, my gosh!" Neil whimpered.

Bob shot a glance at Fred, but Fred was either sleeping or was pretending to. The volunteers called out to one another. Bob smelled coffee and donuts. The murmur of voices in the vast space increased, and the books knew that the sale had opened and customers were trickling in.

"Right, then!" Angela said. "Time to spy a patron. Everyone try to look their best. Let's get on with it."

Bob looked at Fred again. Somehow he seemed nearer. Bob feared Fred would interfere with Angela's plan, though he could hardly imagine Fred would be the type of book that could speak to very many people. Certainly he and Angela wouldn't speak to the same *kinds* of people.

Visitors wandered toward the table where Bob, Angela, and Neil waited. Bob saw Angela watching every likely man who passed. Suddenly he felt a nudge. "That one," Angela said, low and terse. "The blond with the thinning hair and the gym shorts. If he's not an English major, then I'm *Valley of the Dolls*." Her voice became softer, more sweetly insinuating as she called to a young man who stood with his back to their table.

"Hello?" she said. "Been a while since you read a real classic, what? A real good read! Remember what it was like in school? Long evenings reading? All the discoveries?"

Naturally readers cannot hear the actual voices of books, but Angela's ability to communicate with a devoted reader showed. The young man turned, just as a companion came up to him, a shorter, thinner man with thick curly hair and a cheerful manner. Together the two men drifted toward Angela, Bob, and Neil. The blond man had his eye already on the table, as though deep in his brain, down in his memory of himself as a boy fascinated

48

by books, he'd heard Angela. "Marvelous characters!" Angela was saying, in a low and intense voice. "Comedy, suspense, love affairs, that sense that you have found something in life that is yours and only yours, no matter who else may have read it. You remember, don't you? The beauty of the language! The richness! For a couple of dollars you can own something as beautiful as a Tiffany lamp—and more meaningful!"

As Bob watched Angela he realized she was growing more beautiful—not in spite of her age and how used she was, but because of it.

The two men were almost upon them, but Bob also saw Fred looming directly over them. He was tipping forward, about to fall onto all three of them and hide them from view!

But Bob heard a cry of, "Fy! Fy! Ye woll nat prevayle!" He saw a flash of orange and Fred was knocked sideways, as though by the two knights. Fred fell so as to cover Bob and Neil completely, and a good part of Angela, too.

"Blast!" Angela snapped.

"Oops!" said a voice from above. It was the blond man. To one of the volunteers he said, "Your display fell down here." The blond man picked Fred up. Then he looked at his cover. "Oh, yuk!" he said to his friend. "*The Right Way to Live!* I heard this idiot on the radio! No thank you!"

He lowered his voice. "Wait till that volunteer guy looks the other way." The volunteer hurried off to another table. The blond lifted up a stack of four or five hardcover books, slipped Fred underneath, and brought the stack back down hard on top of him. Bob heard Fred's muffled "*Oof!*" This flash of anger worried Bob, for he wanted to like the blond man. After all, Bob thought, he himself had wanted to do the same thing to Fred. And Fred had been horrible to Neil. Meanwhile, the blond man's friend had picked up Sunny. Bob couldn't even look. "Good grief!" the friend said. "I never thought I'd find this!" Bob held his breath. Did everyone in the world think of Sunny as some campy joke? She could be silly, Bob reflected, but she never hurt anyone.

"What's that?" said the blond. "One of those *I'm OK, You're OK*-type things?"

"Kind of," said the friend. "Only this one's really sweet. I had it in college, and I lost it when I moved. It's not great philosophy, but it brings back happy memories. I kept it on my bedside table, and I used to read a paragraph or two every night before going to bed. Very calming. And only a dollar." He took Sunny in hand the way a book buyer does when their decision's been made.

Meanwhile Angela whispered to the blond. "Yes, a classic, a good story, rich, intricate writing, terribly quotable, you can almost see the people and places, you can feel them. And I'm not the Austen people usually read. Not *Pride and Prejudice* or *Sense and Sensibility.* Remember how it used to be when you came on a great book that was a little bit obscure? And you felt you had discovered it and you alone knew about it? Especially when people start carrying on about how they saw the *movie.*"

The blond man picked Angela up. "Speaking of college," he said, "I should really get back to some classics."

"Yes, yes," Angela purred. "But look around, love. How long have you been saying you should find out what the whole 'gay studies' field is about? And it's all sort of, you know, titillating, isn't it? Might recapture a little lost youth for you?"

Bob tried to add a word or two of his own, but found it hard to speak. He had always assumed people were either interested in his specialty or not. Usually not. That he might coax someone to be interested had never occurred to him, and he found he could not do it now. But Angela was doing a fine job for both of them.

"This one really likes to be thoughtful," she said aside to Bob. Then to the blond man she added, "Something scholarly, but fun. It would teach you something. Not some cheap book about husband-hunting or one more political rant."

Bob now felt that maybe he couldn't live up to Angela's billing. He was, after all, a study of pictures of men posing, though Stone made good points about what he called "ico-pornography." Even though Peter had found him interesting and had read him right through, Bob wished he could be a study of a more recognized field, like regular gay history.

The blond man picked Bob up and started to leaf through him. "I've heard that's good," the dark-haired friend said.

"Well," said the blond, "my friend Paulie has the new one, the sequel about porn in the '80s and '90s? He said it wasn't so great, kind of exploitative while it was trying to sound scholarly. The critics said this was the one to read. The guy was really serious when he wrote this, like the pictures are a window onto something."

"And we know how you like those window treatments!" said the friend. "How much?"

"Ten."

"In good condition, too."

Bob felt good hearing that critics liked him more than the Lukes. Pressed secure in the blond man's hand next to Angela, he looked down at Neil and worried. How would Angela pull this off? She had just begun to say, "Now, what about something on the lighter side?" when the blond man said, "Okay, we have a brunch to get to!" and the two of them were off. The two men with their three books wove briskly around tables of more books, hundreds and hundreds unsold, toward the cashier lines at the other end of the Armory.

"Oh dear!" Angela fretted.

"There was nothing you could have done!" Bob said.

"I could have spoken more quickly. Poor Neil! I hope that religious book doesn't resurface and torment him."

Bob expected to hear Sunny, just behind him in the dark-haired man's hand, pipe up with something inspirational about Neil's destiny, but she remained silent. Might she never recover, even when she belonged to a man who appreciated her? Might she never be the same?

"I'd rather be completely out of here!" Angela fretted. "And just know that it simply wasn't possible."

"Try talking to him!" Bob urged.

"Oh, what can I say? Hello? Hello?" She was trying her seductive voice again, but she was too nervous to make it work. Bob tried to call to the man who held him in his hand, but couldn't muster more than a few words, and those did not seem to sink in. Then he called out, "Sunny! Sunny!"

"Ah-ha! Capital idea!" said Angela.

"Hello?" Sunny said in a weak voice. "What is it?"

"Sunny, please, help us!" Bob cried. "We have to get these guys to go back and rescue Neil!"

"Neil?"

"Our friend from the table back there. The book of gay love poems. He's perfect for one of these guys. We wanted him to come with us."

"I'd like to, believe me," Sunny sighed, "but I'm not feeling so inspirational anymore. This fellow's says he likes me, but it's just nostalgia."

"Hurry!" Bob said. "Stop thinking of yourself! We're getting to the front of the line."

"I'm doing my best just telling myself to trust and be positive," Sunny said. "I can't talk to anyone. I don't know who or what I am anymore." The last word was twisted into a little cry.

"Come on, love, just try!" Angela insisted. "This is our friend and you can do the job. Say anything!"

"All right!" Sunny sighed. In a voice weaker than her normal upbeat cries she said, "You fellas know, life isn't all intellectual, all classics and cultural studies. You've got to have a little fun now and then. Something... encouraging!"

"Well," Angela muttered to Bob, "I may not be light, but I like to think of Austen as 'encouraging'!"

"I just hope what she's saying works," Bob added. He had forgotten about his own worries in the mêlée.

"Something written for the heart, from the heart," Sunny continued, now sounding as though the clouds had cleared, as though she'd struck a nerve within herself.

"Once again," Angela muttered, "I'd like to think that I—"

"Oh, dammit!" It was the blond man.

"What?" his friend asked.

"We were going to get Graham some other little thing for his birthday? Remember? We didn't think the espresso pot would be enough."

"You mean we have to go back and find something and stand on line again?"

"No, we can just pick up something back in the neighborhood."

"One of you can go look," Sunny pointed out, "while the other stays in line. The sum is always greater than the parts."

"Poetry!" Bob chimed in. "Poetry's very big right now!" He hissed at Angela. "Isn't it?"

"Yes!" Angela cried suddenly. "Yes! If he likes music he'll like poetry! It inspires the same way. And poetry by gay men for a gay man, why, it will open up a huge horizon for him!" To Bob she whispered, "God, I'm beginning to sound like the other one, aren't I?"

Meanwhile, Sunny was crying out to the dark-haired one: "Something inspirational! Something to make your friend feel the way I always made you feel before turning out the light!" Bob began feeding Sunny a description of Neil.

"Wait," the dark-haired one said. "You know, back on that table there was this little book of gay love poems."

"You think Graham would go for that?" asked the blond, making a face.

"YES!" Bob, Angela, and Sunny cried out together.

"Yes," said the dark-haired man. "I'll run back and get it. A little book like that is good to have around for anyone, anytime."

The blond man agreed, so his friend set off to find Neil. In less than a minute he returned.

"Gone," he said.

Bob and Angela and Sunny gasped.

"Oh, well," said the blond.

By that time they were almost to the checkout.

Sunny moaned and Bob felt his heart break.

"Are you sure?" Angela demanded. "Did you look carefully?"

"I looked everywhere," the dark-haired man told the blond.

"It doesn't matter," said the blond. "We'll get Graham some other little thing."

And soon the two men had paid, and they and their three books were out in the sunlight, briskly moving eastward. (Bob had a bookmark stuck in him that he found most irritating.)

"Oh, poor, dear Neil!" Angela fretted. "I didn't like the look of that religious book, not at all. And what if the Malory gets sold? What can we ever do now?"

"Trust, I guess," Sunny said. She sounded neither overly upbeat nor depressed. She sounded peaceful and a little sad. "Just trust. We are not in control of this. Whatever's going to happen has already been decided. That is the beauty of it all, I suppose."

The two men walked on toward their brunch.

Chapter 5
Inclusion/Exclusion

The blond man turned out to be named Alfred; his shorter, darker friend was Ron. Angela, Bob, and Sunny spent a pleasant sidewalk brunch with them and their two friends. Pleasant for the men, that is. The books fretted, though Sunny's advice calmed them somewhat. "We should at least be grateful we're not back there," she said.

"But it's hard to enjoy our luck," Bob complained, "when Neil could be in so much trouble." Angela agreed.

Later, the men brought their books back to a narrow brick apartment building in the East 80s, off Third Avenue. Bob, Angela, and Sunny ascertained that, while Ron and Alfred shared the apartment, they were not boyfriends. "They should've taken the love poetry," Bob wanted to say, though he knew what Sunny's answer would be: "Everything in it's time." Bob disliked comforting slogans. He preferred Angela's practicality.

Ron did not take Sunny to his bedside table just yet, so the three friends were able to stay together a little longer. Ron left

Sunny by a chair with a bright if uninspiring view—the backs of other buildings, fire escapes, and the occasional patch of ivy. Alfred put Angela and Bob on the wide arm of an easy chair in a corner with a smaller window, some geraniums, and a lamp. Both men had plans other than reading for that afternoon, so the three books had a chance to look around at their new companions—hundreds more books, mostly belonging to Alfred, arranged on shelves up to the ceiling.

Angela quickly felt at home. Most of Alfred's books were paperback classics, many with covers similar to hers. Alfred owned no *Tristram Shandy*, but he did own other Austen novels, several by Dickens and the Brontës, and many twentieth-century British authors and American classics. Bob could stand back and observe their personalities, as they mostly left him out of conversations they had with Angela. He had expected *Wuthering Heights* to speak rapturously and romantically, for that's what he'd always heard about the book. Yet Perry, Alfred's copy of *Wuthering Heights*, was brutish. Bob had expected *Huckleberry Finn* to be upbeat and simple, yet Alfred's copy, a dog-eared fellow named Jake, had a complex personality: droll, at times reverent, or outspoken, playful or thoughtful. Bob didn't know what to think of him. Few of Alfred's books understood who Bob was. Alfred had read gay novels, but while he had long wondered what he might glean from "gay studies," he'd never bought a scholarly book on the subject. Even now he told Ron that he felt odd having purchased a book that dealt with gay photo sets and pornography, instead of some political or social issue. This made Bob feel more vulnerable in front of Alfred's classic novels. Those classics had some rapport with Alfred's gay fiction, because Edward, a paperback copy of E. M. Forster's *Maurice*, had made it his business to mediate, as it were, between the classics, and more modern works of Neil Bartlett, David Leavitt, and Andrew Holleran. Alfred also owned some lesbian classics—by Radclyffe Hall, Djuna Barnes, and others—and the strait-laced, older books took less issue with these.

The young men in tank tops on the covers of the gay male novels made books with old master paintings feel uncomfortable, though the gay novels often expressed dissatisfaction with their own covers. To Bob's surprise, some classics said the same thing. One thick nineteenth-century novel with a painting of a sunny meadow and undulating hills complained, "As though it were all croquet and flower arrangements! They never show the passion in me!"

Bob surveyed the walls and tried to find some book who might find him interesting, and when he couldn't, his thoughts turned back to Moishe. He hoped Moishe lived now with sympathetic souls, and that his owner had marked him up and annotated him as he had always wished. And what of poor Neil, who did not look as though he could withstand another onslaught from *The Right Way to Live*? Bob hoped that Neil had simply been bought by another book lover, a few seconds after Bob himself had been taken. Even if he had, though, Bob could not help think what close calls they had endured and might endure again. And what of that religious book? Was it fair that Alfred should have buried it so far down? *Would anyone ever buy it and really be interested in it?* And the orange-covered book—who would love a book that would be so difficult to read? A certain kind of scholar would have to find it.

After a while, Angela struck up a conversation with Bob about how the day had turned out. Bob wanted the other books to see his friendship with Angela and accept him more. On the other side of the room, Sunny waited quietly to be opened. Her faith had begun to fade. *It happens,* she thought, *in spite of all you try to tell yourself. People grab you for a dollar out of nostalgia, but they don't really go back and read you, and when they move or spring clean, the impulse fades.* Sunny decided she should prepare herself for a life of being sold and resold. If she were lucky. What if Ron just one day threw her out with the egg shells and coffee grounds? She'd seen it happen.

Meanwhile, Neil was indeed safe. A few seconds after Alfred took Bob and Angela, another man took Neil. Neil had endured a scary interlude when that man tossed him back. Instead of placing him back on his original table, with the gallant orange-covered Malory, the man had tossed him onto a table of police thrillers. None mocked Neil outright, but the looks they gave and the few words they spoke let him know they did not welcome him. They suggested he'd be happier on another table, but said no more. Neil began to think it was his fault that he had landed there. Just then, though, a volunteer saw the incongruity and rescued Neil. The volunteer found a more sympathetic table, with some literary novels and a picture book on gardening. There Neil settled in, but briefly. A nervous man in his early twenties picked Neil up, held him in both hands, leafed through him with an intense gaze, and added him to the stack in his hand.

Angela's ability to speak to readers had fascinated Neil. The speaking itself presented no problem for him. He was not tongue-tied, like Bob. But when the nervous young man, Owen, got Neil home, and Neil tried to speak, he saw perplexing results. Owen would look at Neil—longingly, Neil thought—and Neil would say, "Come on, dip in, read a few." Neil believed that Owen heard him, but instead of picking Neil up and reading, Owen turned away with a stony look, a deliberately defeated, angry expression Neil did not understand. Still, he did not throw Neil out. He kept him out, he looked at him several times a day, but he never answered Neil's call to read the love poetry inside. Neil supposed that he understood why Owen was, as Neil ascertained after a few days, single.

Neil could not help noticing other books owned by Owen. His library consisted of three broad categories: books of psychology: Freud, Jung, Reich, Kübler-Ross, and others; books of plays; and books on what might be called gay husband-hunting. Neil expected this last category to speak as Sunny had. In truth, their upbeat tone was compromised by something of the mood into which Sunny had fallen after the young couple mocked her. The husband-hunting books said over and over that Owen had to "have confidence in himself" and "be open." They could not converse about topics other than what was in their pages. They were both inspirational and humorless. *How could that be?* They were also single, continually finding fault with one another and with Owen's other books. They were not urbane, as the psychology books were, nor inventive, like the plays. The husband-hunting books doubted the romance expressed in Neil's poems. One even went so far as to call Neil "useless," though he later apologized. Yet the psychology texts, educated as they were, spoke too analytically. Neil couldn't understand Owen's personality based on what his books said. Consequently, Neil turned to the one category left. He would see what the plays had to say.

"He is so terribly, awfully lonely," trilled a nervous book named Annabelle. Her title was *Collected Plays of Tennessee Williams, Vol. 3.* "I declare, when he's with a man, he's more lonely than when he is without one. When it is summer and he dresses in white, why he is a vision, yet he is so terribly lonely."

"Well doth he play the part of vision," said Owen's *Complete Shakespeare.* "Yet visionary he is not, for were he to be a visionary man, he would think less to play the part of vision, and more to seek his vision in another."

"Thus, thus, is Owen fallen!" cried *Selected Greek Tragedies.* "Weep, Manhattan, for Owen, thy fallen son! Seek him not in thy piano bars, but alone at Armani Exchange! Seek him alone before his closet, in lonely quest for a more fabulous outfit!"

"For when he sits at his toilet," remarked *Wycherly: Selected Comedies,* "then does he look into his mirror and see there the only man upon who he may keep his affection. Then does he become hardened, and in hardening becomes blind, for hardness shall always shut up the sight, until that thing is discharged which hath caused the hardness!"

"Oh!" exclaimed Annabelle. "I cannot bear such rude talk! You are an awful, vulgar volume!"

The Wycherly smirked and responded, "Methinks 'tis roughness the lady doth crave, and that the lady doth wax angrily because that roughness is only in the thrust of the talk and not, as 'twere, in the thrust itself!"

Owen apparently liked musicals, too, for he owned a shelf of Gilbert and Sullivan scores, who chimed in with their opinions. One of them sang:

"When this young man goes out on a date
To seek the lad who might be his soul mate
He finds not goodness but instead sees faults
And when the evening's over he goes back to the Vault!"

To which the others added:

"Yes, when the evening's over he goes back to the Vault!"

The first book sang:

"He stays so long in these sleazy haunts,
That now he's lost all sight of what he really wants!"

And the others echoed:

"He stays so long in these sleazy haunts,
That now he's lost all sight of what he really wants!"

What a strange limbo, Neil reflected, being a book of love poems that belonged to a man who, from what these volumes said and from what he himself had observed, refused to give or to receive love. Why had Owen purchased him? In order to feel worse? Neil thought of Owen building a wall around himself—with a book of love poems, paradoxically as the keystone. But keystones belonged to arches. (As a book of poetry, Neil loved such whimsical associations.) Maybe Owen did have a doorway somewhere.

Neil found some consolation and enlightenment from a book named Marc. Marc's title was *It's a Fine Life: Queer Connections in a Modern World.* Marc was curious and intelligent and his text went beyond husband-hunting to talk about "families of choice." He had what Neil thought was an invigorating annoyance with husband-hunting books. "Owen goes out on these dates trying to look and act perfect," Marc said, "but he's certain underneath that he's not perfect. At the same time he's looking for someone who is. And guess what his feeling is about that someone, the moment they sit down to dinner?"

"Not perfect, either," Neil concluded.

"Score one for you," Marc said. "He wants this kind of perfect parent, and I have a theory—I mean, literally, I have this theory in my first chapter, how good lovers are to a great extent good parents. Part of being a lover is this kind of parenting function."

"Wait," Neil said. "Didn't Owen get any of this from reading you?"

"Oh?" Marc said. "You don't think he's read me, do you? This friend of his gave me to him a year ago. Do I look like I've been opened? I might as well be back in the store. Fortunately, I like Gilbert and Sullivan, or it'd be a total waste living here!"

"Hey, you want to talk about total wastes?"

Neil and Marc looked. Another husband-hunting book had spoken: *How to Find (and Keep) that Perfect Mate, A Guide for Gay Men,* by Alowicious Council, Ph.D. The book's name was Howie.

"He read me in one afternoon," Howie complained. "I made him feel better, but in that high kind of way, like everything's magically resolved. It wore off and by evening he was restless again. He bought that guy over there, *Meeting and Mating, Advice for the Gay Man,* three days later. Same thing happened to him. I only hope we're as lucky as you"—Howie nodded toward

Neil—"and get recycled through a book sale. Sometimes he turns on us. He gets disgusted and throws some of us out."

Neither Marc nor Neil spoke. Neil wondered, would his love poems set off similar strong emotions and resentments in Owen? Already Owen seemed to disdain him, after grasping him so intensely at the book sale. Neil thought he could not bear to be tossed in the trash, head down amongst the coffee grounds and apple cores Sunny dreaded. To spend eternity rotting in a landfill? If that were to be his future, he would almost wish he'd been burned in Alabama. At least then he might be with Jerry right now in some book Heaven. Jerry had fought. Neil knew he had, and he was proud of him for it. *But how much could a book fight? Others were in charge. They would burn you or shred you, and their lives went on.* As he tried to sleep that night, Neil fretted. He tried to forget his worries by remembering how Jerry had bucked him up when he was low, before the burning, as the books were gathered in the church basement. *Did Jerry know?* Did he know how bad it would be, and did he protect Neil precisely because it was hopeless? Neil glanced at Marc, snoring gently. Marc seemed nice. And maybe Owen never would read him, would never read either of them, and they could just keep to themselves and be friends. That would be ideal.

Back at Alfred and Ron's apartment, Alfred spent evenings reading Bob and Angela alternately. Bob felt jealous that Alfred spent more time with Angela, and that he had told Ron when he'd finished her, he was going back to all his other Austen novels. But Bob also knew what Sunny, now on Ron's bedside table, would say: Bob should make the most of what he had. Alfred read him regularly, and Bob could feel Alfred's interest as he read. Alfred even marked some parts with asterisks. Not the kind of close study Moishe had dreamed of, but Bob felt he had something of value to say.

"What's this?" Alfred called to Ron the next afternoon, picking a colorful flyer out of the mail.

"It's a conference on gay writing in Boston," Ron said.

"And Harrison Stone will be there!" Alfred added, reading the flyer. "The author of this book I bought, remember?" He rushed over and picked up Bob, and Bob listened with great interest.

"That's why I saved the flyer for you," Ron said. "D'you want to go? Christopher Bram and Patrick Merla are speaking on the future of the gay novel, and Stone on gay imagery. Maybe you could bring Stone's book and get an autograph."

"Well!" exclaimed Angela from the cocktail table. "An autograph! Something I can never have!"

"We'll see if they end up going," Bob murmured. He hoped they would, as Alfred read more of him that evening. *An autograph!* Bob thought.

And then he wished that, wherever he was, Moishe could have an autograph, too.

Chapter 6
The Conference

Alfred and Ron made plans to attend the gay writing conference. Day by day Alfred read more of Angela, closing in on the ending, so she feared she would not be coming to Boston. Bob would have to go without his best friend.

"I'll be cheering for you, though," Angela promised. "An autograph—my, my!"

The two men drove to Boston on a sunny Friday in early March. Ron had the passenger window open. Alfred placed Bob on the dashboard, with a perfect, panoramic of the highway and the rising towers of the city. Bob thought about more than the view, however. This conference tormented him. He could not ignore the hope, more powerful than reason, that Moishe would show up. But he could not ignore reason, either: Moishe almost certainly would not be there. That woman, who Bob had perceived as straight, had taken Moishe from him months ago. She must have purchased Moishe for scholarly purposes, and this conference did not sound scholarly to Bob. Serious, yes, but not full of Ph.D.s.

The excitement of downtown Boston overcame the tug-of-war in Bob's mind: tall, mirrored skyscrapers and reckless, swooping traffic, the marble grandeur of the hotel, the warm sparkle of chandeliers. Men and women registered for rooms and for seminars and lectures. A cocktail hour had begun on the hotel's mezzanine. Gay and lesbian magazines lay out on display, many with tantalizing pictures. Bob felt lonely now. Alfred, assuming he would buy books at the conference, had brought no other volumes with him. Ron had brought only a Boston guide book, Mike, who was something of a bore. He acted gay, talking about things one "*had* to see," that were "tucked away" or "just a quick walk" from one another, but if he were asked about his few gay and lesbian listings, he changed the subject to minutemen or the Red Sox or his girlfriend, a guidebook to Montréal that Ron just happened to have lent long term to a friend. While Alfred and Ron enjoyed cocktails on the mezzanine, Bob had to lie in Alfred's room listening to Mike drone on about Old Ironsides and about how beautiful his girlfriend's cover was.

The next day proved more intriguing. Harrison Stone's talk would take place in the morning, and Bob would get his autograph. Bob had thought of the autographing only abstractly up to that point. Now it did seem momentous, as Angela had said. This was something Angela could not have. Bob had a living author and she did not. The excitement over the autograph blinded Bob. He had imagined himself and dozens of other Bobs being autographed together—a grand celebration. He had forgotten the Lukes.

Reviewers said the new book, *A Mirror Crack'd*, served two functions for the men who read it. It looked scholarly, for Stone analyzed the "representations" in great detail. But the publishers had insisted that Stone include many more photographs, most in color, and the men in these photos, gay porn icons of recent times, were more to the taste of contemporary gay readers. It was like porn, in a tasteful, unassailable form. Men exchanged copies of this book at birthday and holiday parties, while concealing their nudging, winking motives. Stone's new book was at once a juicy gag and a must-have, and the hotel banquet room where Stone would speak was crowded with men in jeans and black T-shirts, with tans and chain-like bracelets, clutching Lukes for autographs.

From where Alfred sat, Bob could not see one single other Bob. Maybe Stone wouldn't deign to autograph his old book. He must love the Lukes more, with their creamy photographs and their best seller status. The Lukes had made Stone wealthy, and Bob figured he loved them for that. Stone gave a talk with slides, many of which provoked chuckles from the men in the audience. Bob could not see the slides from Alfred's lap, and he decided he didn't want to. Bob could tell from what Stone said that the early nudes played a smaller part in the slide show. Stone even said, "I'll just hurry through these so we can take a look at what you really came to see!" And the men laughed.

"Now we get to the real goodies!" Stone announced. While Bob could not see the slides, he could look up and see the colorful glow that filled the room as several of the men exclaimed "Ooooh!" under their breath, and giggled. Alfred readjusted himself in his seat. Bob could tell he was getting an erection. He'd had a few while reading Bob, and Bob had felt particularly gratified that Alfred had never bought the new book. He probably would now, though, and Bob would have to live forever with one of the Lukes, shallow, self-satisfied fellows who had referred to him as Stone's "old book," with "old photos" from the "olden days."

The men clapped enthusiastically when the lecture ended and the lights came on again. Stone took a few questions, but it was time for the next lecture to begin. A small, quiet group of women waited outside the door for the next event. As the men rose to go, Alfred quickly made his way to the front. Bob liked Alfred for caring so much about Stone's "old" book.

"Ah! The original!" Stone exclaimed when he saw Bob. "I am more than happy to sign this for you," he said, uncapping his fountain pen, "This is the one that means the most to me. The publishers ruined the new one, frankly. People buy it just to leer, but I commend you for reading this one. This one is the closest to my heart."

Bob felt gratified to hear this, but his pride was soon undercut. The stack of Luke's to Stone's left immediately chorused, "Uh-huh!" and "Oh, sure!" and "One word, Miss Stone: 'royalties'!" Men were picking the Lukes up and leafing through them. Lukes didn't worry much about others' opinions, even their author's, because the world loved them and wanted them nonstop. If their own author called them shallow, what did that matter next to all these handsome men's hands all over them, oohing, aahing, pointing, desiring, paying?

Bob decided he preferred Stone's strong but soft hands on him, deliberately turning pages to get to the title page, caressing the paper and taking his time with his pen strokes. Bob could feel his author's appreciation and he sighed with gratitude. But then he saw Alfred was buying a Luke! "I want to see for myself," he told Stone.

"Oh, by all means," Stone said. "I always like to sell more books. Pays for that house in the south of France!"

Alfred grinned and nodded. He put the two books together in his left hand.

"*Hmmm*," the new Luke said to Bob, "you're the old book."

"The *original*," Bob said, then casting about for something he could say that would make him feel as good as Luke. "I was just autographed," he added.

"Me too," Luke said.

"I didn't see him autograph you," Bob said.

"That was before."

"Before what?"

"We were autographed before," Luke said severely.

Bob still didn't understand, but he didn't think he should say any more. Just then he caught the words of an assistant, working next to Stone.

"All pre-autographed!" the assistant told the men gathered round the table, as he plunked down a fresh stack of Lukes. "Pre-autographed, let's keep it moving, the girls want to get in!"

After Stone's lecture, Alfred attended a seminar on gay literary anthologies, then met Ron for lunch at a pizzeria a block from the hotel. Afternoon presentations would not begin for another two hours, so after eating, the two men came back to a hotel conference room containing tables of gay merchandise. Most prominent, of course, were books—books from small publishers, independent presses, even a display of used and rare gay and lesbian titles. Ron and Alfred wove through the room, taking copies of catalogues, and examining titles from independent presses. Next to the rare and used section, Alfred put Bob and Luke down in order to try on a rainbow amulet on a leather cord. He decided against it, but just as he put it back, Ron called to Alfred from another spot in the room. Bob was disconcerted when Alfred dashed off without him. Luke, meanwhile, was irritated.

The way Alfred had set them down, Luke was on the bottom, and Bob heard him mutter, "Well, no one can see my cover like this!" Alfred and Ron continued browsing on to the other side of the room, moving further and further away! Even if Bob could speak to people as easily as Angela, Alfred was too far away to hear him. He'd forgotten him! And Luke was having his little hissy fit. Bob realized that Luke didn't care. If Alfred forgot him altogether, someone would grab him and pass him around. Bob barely had time to worry about his abandonment, though, because suddenly he smelled smoke. *A fire in the hotel?* He looked every which way. No one else seemed to smell it. People laughed and chatted and perused books as though nothing were happening. But Bob smelled smoke. *Definitely.*

With a start Bob noticed a dignified used book with a white cover with a photograph of three men. The title read, *Christianity and Homosexuality: A New Perspective*, by Reverend Jeremiah Lott. The photo showed a middle-aged man—Reverend Lott?—with his arms around the shoulders of two handsome young men, one to his left, one to his right, who were holding hands. The smoky smell came from this book. The book showed little interest in anything going on around him. Its silent dignity made Bob think of the orange book with the knights at the Armory. Bob actually hoped that Alfred would take his time, for this book intrigued him.

"Forgive me for staring," Bob said.

"It's the smell, isn't it?" the book said.

Bob remembered something. "Were you—if you don't mind my asking—were you in a fire?" he asked.

"Yes," the book said. "I should be thankful I'm alive." He paused. "I was in a book burning."

Bob felt shivery all over. "Where?"

"Alabama. Fortunately I wound up on the bottom, and then they made them put the fire out because they didn't—"

"Do you know Neil?" Bob asked.

The other book went silent.

"You're Jerry!" Bob said.

The book said nothing.

"I know Neil," Bob said. "We were in a book sale together and he told me about you. He loves you very much but he thinks you're dead. I wish I knew where he was now. We tried to get sold together but it didn't work."

The book still could not speak.

"You still love Neil, don't you, Jerry?"

Now here was Alfred, coming toward them. How could Bob get Alfred to buy this book? Alfred was not religious, as far as Bob knew. Most gay men weren't, although many Bob had met said they were "spiritual." And Bob wasn't good at speaking to people, but he tried now as Alfred swooped down.

"Here they are!" Alfred called. He picked up Bob and Luke and turned to go. Luke grunted disconsolately. It occurred to Bob that Luke had actually hoped to be abandoned. Then he could have the pleasure of being discovered and desired by someone new.

Bob tried to protest, to yell something to make Alfred stop and consider Jerry. But Alfred had turned away from the used books and was rushing back to Ron.

Chapter 7
Many and Various Encounters

While Bob was away with Alfred, Neil was being read by Owen. Owen picked Neil up one evening after he found nothing he wanted to watch on TV. As far as Neil could tell, no event had motivated Owen to read love poetry—no date, no new prospective lover. On the other hand, there was no particular despair, no recent evening (as sometimes there had been) when Owen dressed up and put on cologne at seven, then came home stony-faced at one or two in the morning and drank wine in front of the television. Owen picked Neil up on an ordinary night. He did not read sequentially. Neil could tell (for books can feel the heat of their readers' gazes going over their lines) that Owen did not finish most of the poems. He'd get three-quarters of the way through and flip to another. He read, but did not finish, a verse by Sappho, then he skipped to the contemporary poets at the end of the book. But their messages did not satisfy him, either.

Then he swung back to Shakespeare, managing an entire sonnet because, Neil guessed, one had to finish Shakespeare—

because he's Shakespeare. (Neil's editor had included Shakespeare on the strength of the rumor that he was bisexual.)

Then Owen stared into space. His hand hung over the arm of the chair. Neil dangled perilously. He cried out to Owen to wake up, but of all the books Owen owned, Owen could hear only the plays, and even those had grown faint within the past few years. When the psychology or husband-hunting books spoke to Owen, he heard something, but what he heard rarely matched what the books were saying.

Now some of the drama books noticed Neil's precarious position and cried out. But they could not break Owen's trance, and then his eyes shut. One book opined that Owen went to sleep not in spite of the cries of his drama books, but because of them. He did not want to remember his days in the theatre. He did not want to think that leaving the theatre might have been a mistake, or be reminded that he had yet to find a satisfactory life away from it. So the voices of theatre books only made him crave sleep. And sleep he did, and when he shifted he dropped Neil—*bump!* on his binding—and then turned and curled up, knees pulled to his chest, in the chair.

"Are you all right?" called Marc, Owen's unread copy of *It's a Fine Life: Queer Connections in a Modern World.*

"I think so," Neil said. "I'm light. It didn't hurt too much. I only hope he picks me up again."

The husband-hunting books chuckled ruefully. "Not likely," one of them said. Neil could tell this book spoke out of his own bitterness, not pessimism for Neil's prospects.

"Finishing books is a problem for him," Marc said. "Especially books on love or commitment. And of course he's never even started me."

"We've got to get out of here," remarked a book called *Dating and Mating in the Gay '90s*. "Get sold before we start to yellow and our covers get ripped. Find someone who can use us."

"For what?" asked a book called *Getting Together, Staying Together*. "Most of the guys who buy us—or people who buy straight versions of us—aren't going to take the advice we put in front of their faces. You yellow on the shelf and if you're lucky get resold."

"And at the used-book store, no one buys you," *Dating and Mating* added. "they assume you didn't work out for someone. Never that you did, that you helped someone find a mate and so you could be passed on with a sense of giving."

"Just try being given or taken as a gift," said another husband-hunting book. "Usually you're bought surreptitiously. Some guys are more comfortable buying porn than buying us."

"We've gotta get out of this place," *Getting Together* insisted. "The only problem is how."

"Take me with you?" Neil asked. "Please?"

"Sure," Marc said. "If we can get out. We can't suggest it to him. He doesn't listen to us. There's no book in this apartment that can speak directly to him. We have to hang on and hope."

"And hope we're sold," Neil said. "Not trashed."

"Don't even think it!" Marc said.

Neil thought of Sunny, always thinking positively, or trying to, until she was treated so badly by the couple at the Armory. Neil hoped he and Marc and the others could keep their spirits up until Owen gave them a second chance in the world.

📖

"Did you hear him lecture?"

Alfred turned. "Excuse me?"

The young man watching the used and rare book table repeated his question: "Did you hear him lecture this morning? He indicated Bob. "Harrison Stone?"

Alfred noticed now how appealing this fellow looked. He noticed how the fellow had not merely asked a question, but had fixed him with a hazel-eyed look that asked for more than a chat about Harrison Stone. Alfred reapproached the table.

"Yes," he said. "I did."

"I wanted to go," said the young man, "but I'd promised to work here and there was no one else. You know how the literary world is. Everyone spread so thin." He extended his hand to Alfred. "Duane," he said. Alfred shook hands. "Alfred," he said.

Meanwhile Bob, nestled under Alfred's arm, was trying desperately to get Alfred to buy Jerry. Bob couldn't begin to think how to find Neil. But if he could get Alfred to buy Jerry, one piece of the puzzle would be in place. Without Jerry, all would be lost.

Bob tried to remember how Angela had persuaded Alfred to buy her. She promised a wonderful story and characters, and she had gotten Alfred to buy Bob, too, with promises of scholarly enlightenment. How could Bob transfer this to Jerry? Bob, as a scholarly book, thought he did not have the gifts of seduction that Angela had. And Luke, pressed beside Bob under Alfred's arm, was no help.

"Try something new!" Bob yelled, unable to imagine any other reason Alfred should buy a book on Christianity and homosexuality.

"A used book?" Luke complained. "Oh, please! And a book on *Christianity*? Give me one good reason!"

"Shut up!" Bob cried. "This is important. I know his boyfriend. Maybe we can get them back together! Jerry, say something!"

"As if!" said Luke. "God, I wish this guy would hold me so my cover would show!"

Alfred and Duane continued to chat. Alfred, just to keep the conversation going, spoke of the books on the table. This relieved Duane, who could talk for hours about books, but who became tongue-tied over questions about his personal life.

When Alfred looked down at the books spread out between them, he immediately fell silent. Bob sensed the tension and became quiet, too. Even Luke seemed momentarily interested.

Bob could tell by the tension in Alfred's body that he was remembering something emotional.

"Wow," Alfred said softly.

Duane asked, "What is it?"

"This book—"

"This one?" Duane briefly gave the book's history, especially the book burning. Alfred seemed only to half-hear it. "When I was in college," Alfred interrupted, "I kind of... liked this one guy."

Bob could see Alfred was being careful in how the phrased things to Duane, who watched Alfred, intrigued. Alfred continued. "But he was in a Christian fellowship organization and he did say he liked me, too, but—"

"But it was a sin," Duane said.

"Not quite. He believed it was 'okay for some people,' but he wanted a family, he didn't want to be lonely, and he thought all gay men just cruised in parks."

"Courtesy of Doctor Reuben," Duane said.

"Exactly. I thought I could change his mind. So at the end of the spring semester I bought this book and gave it to him. I planned it for weeks. It took a lot for me to buy something like this back then, but the cashier didn't bat an eye."

"Probably queer himself."

"I didn't know about stuff like that then."

By now Alfred had Jerry in his hand. "I remember wanting this guy to at least hug me or something when I gave it to him. I was also afraid he'd be repulsed and never speak to me again. But neither happened. He took it, thanked me, said it looked 'interesting.' I didn't hear from him all summer. In the fall he greeted me as though nothing had ever happened between us. It was eerie."

"Did he ever get married?" Duane asked.

"He got a girlfriend that year," said Alfred. "I don't think the girlfriend lasted. They looked awkward together."

"Ain't it the way?" Duane said.

Alfred opened Jerry's cover and checked the price.

"So you're still kind of attached to him?" Duane asked.

"Oh, no!" Alfred said. "That was years ago. But I'm curious. I never read this myself. I tried to be patient with him, but in my head I dismissed everything he had to say about his religion, especially vis-à-vis homosexuality. Maybe I should find out. Plus the story you told me about this book. I love a book with a history and that's quite a story, about the book burning. By 'Christians,' no less!"

Duane agreed that it was quite a story. Alfred paid him for the book. Finally he asked Duane, "Do they ever give you a break from this?"

Duane said the merchandise tables closed at six. Alfred suggested dinner, and Duane agreed. Bob could see Ron in the background, watching with a little, sad smile on his face. Alfred brought Ron forward and introduced him. Alfred called Ron "my buddy" very clearly. Duane beamed and shook Ron's hand, then finalized dinner plans with Alfred.

"So, we have something developing here?" Ron said as they strolled away.

Alfred grinned. "Maybe."

"Oh my God!" Luke hissed, there under Alfred's arm, beside Bob and the new book. "That smell! What is it?"

"Weren't you listening?" Bob demanded. "Jerry, here, was in a book burning!"

"Oh," Luke said. "Gee."

"So you did know Neil, didn't you?" Bob asked Jerry.

"I knew Neil, yes," Jerry said softly. "Now and then I see other copies of that book. But never my Neil. You said you saw him, though?"

Bob told about meeting Neil at the Armory, and the plan they'd had with Angela, and how it had failed. Bob commiserated with Jerry, telling the story of how he had become separated from Moishe.

While Jerry and Bob talked, Luke just took deep breaths. Finally, at a break in the conversation, he said, "So, like, what exactly is a 'book burning'?"

Chapter 8
Trouble, Past and Present

Bob got to know Jerry better that evening, alone in Alfred and Ron's hotel room. Ron had taken the T to Cambridge, and Alfred had gone out with Duane to a vegetarian restaurant. In the hotel room Bob heard the story of Jerry's life: his being printed and shipped to the small gay bookstore in Alabama, the vandalism and cruelties he witnessed there, and his falling in love with Neil. Bob told Jerry about Angela and how she had tried to get Alfred to buy the two of them, and Neil, too, but had failed.

"Poor thing," Jerry said, when Bob told him about how Neil had endured the harsh environment of the Armory book sale, then been left alone. "He always had trouble going it alone. It would have been so much better if he'd been bought along with you and your friend. But you couldn't do anything. Sometimes people hear us, sometimes not. I've worried so much about him. By the time I was dug out from the bottom of that book burning, the rest of the unburned books were gone. I called for Neil, many of us called for our loved ones, but when I heard no answer I knew either he had been burned, or he'd never gotten to the fire and would be disposed of some other way. I'd never see him again. I prayed he'd escaped. I thought I'd never know, so I have to thank you for telling me he's alive... I just hope he finds someone. He'll never know I'm alive. Why would he even think it?"

"So wait," said Luke. "Like, what happened to you guys? I mean, you gotta know you got this kind of rank smell. I'm just saying. Cards on the table, here."

"It was terrible," Jerry said bitterly, eyeing Luke. "I don't know if I can make you understand, but I will try. We were used to little incidents at the bookstore. Someone came in the night and spray-painted 'FAG' across the door, and the proprietor got threatening phone calls. We could hear them all the way up on the shelves—'You dirty so-and-so'—and the police never did anything, or they came and made wisecracks and said the owner was 'inviting it' by selling gay books.

"So most of the time no one even bothered reporting an incident. Sometimes someone would slip a note under the door. We'd hear it in the middle of the night, scraping the carpet. One day this man came in. In a black suit and a narrow tie. He stood with his hands behind his back and looked around with the most hateful expression. He had thin lips, big, shaggy eyebrows, and creases in his pants sharp as knives.

"The boy behind the counter said, 'May I help you?' and the man just went on casting his eye around like he could tear us apart right there. Then he stepped over to a shelf, grabbed two handfuls of books, plunked them down on the counter and took out his wallet. The boy said, 'Do you want to buy these?'

"The man said nothing. The boy pointed out that the man had two copies of the same books. The man said nothing. He paid, took the books, and left. The next day he came again and did the same thing. Only the next day, a woman came, too, with a huge hairdo and too much makeup, vicious-looking like the man, and she also grabbed two fistfuls of books, without looking, and bought them.

"Well, the rumors flew. We didn't have many used books there, so no one knew the kinds of horrors that went on outside the store. We heard the owner on the phone. He was debating with friends whether to refuse to sell anything more to these people. Finally, he did. The man came in a day later and the owner said, 'Your money's not good here, sir.' The man turned and went. We didn't know what could be going on.

"Two days later another man came in. He spoke strangely, exaggeratedly, doing a bad impersonation of a gay man. He chose some books and was saying, '*Oh!* I can't wait to read *this* one!' The owner was not there, and what could he have done anyway? That gay impersonation was more sinister than the silence of the first guy. Then there were others, every day, two or three times a day. They all felt phony, faces trying to look friendly and then suddenly they had these awful black lasers coming out of their eyes.

"Finally, two came in together. We heard them whispering, one saying, 'Doesn't it make you sick?' and the other saying, 'I will praise the Lord the day these all go up in flames!' What did that mean? We'd never heard of book burnings, but by then this one used book lived there with us who gave us some idea. We just didn't want to believe him. Neil and I clung to each other and waited. We questioned the books on shelves closest to those two people, but they hadn't heard anything more. No one would say anything because they feared things would be worse if we schemed or resisted.

"These people kept coming back. The owner reordered, but our shelves were getting emptier. The owner felt ambivalent, because he was making a ton of money. At one point he actually said, 'Hey, there's no such thing as bad publicity!'

"Then they took Neil and me. We'd prayed to be taken together. In a way it was a relief when it finally happened. We were bought, taken outside, took a perfectly normal car ride, it all looked fine. The book burning idea was ridiculous...

"Then we saw the steeple, like a knife in the sky. They unloaded us, stuffed us down in a basement, and there they were! All our friends from the store. Everyone greeted us and wept. They'd heard the same thing. 'We're going to die!' they cried. 'We're going to burn!' And of course the church people heard none of these cries.

"We spent the next few days huddled together, praying, weeping, hoping something might happen, as more and more of our comrades arrived, more of us stuffed weeping and shivering into that basement. Three days later, at twilight, we saw through the basement window: the men building the tower of wood, rising in front of the church, dark and crooked, something evil that the little white steeple was powerless to fight. Night fell. We waited. Men circled the tower, throwing liquid from cans. Cars pulled up. Dozens of people got out, then hundreds. All of a sudden it was dark, and they came with torches and touched them to the bottom. We saw the flames catch and rise, twisting, gigantic. More cars came, headlight beams waving wildly. Suddenly the basement door was flung open. The men came down, their footsteps thundering. They grabbed us roughly in armfuls and tossed us in wheelbarrows and wheeled us out where all those hundreds of people were standing around, stony-faced like that man on that first day. Their dark eyes that reflected little pinpoints of firelight. They held signs: 'FAGS BURN IN HELL!' and 'GOD HATES QUEERS!'

"And that first man was there, wearing a clerical collar. He grabbed one of us, his name was Scott, he was a copy of *The Joy of Gay Sex*. He had—he had become—my friend in those few days—the minister grabbed him off the top of the wheelbarrow, held him up, announced his title to the crowd, and said, 'There will be no more joy for sinners!' And he tossed Scott onto the fire as the crowd cheered so loudly it drowned out his screams.

"After that he took one after another of us, announced each title and threw us into the flames. I watched my friends sail through the air, screaming, into the inferno. One moment they were with us, the next they were gone. I prayed I'd go before Neil, that I wouldn't have to watch him be held up and hear the minister say awful things about him." Jerry took a deep breath and paused. "I thought, in my case, that my title would give them pause. Poor Neil. They'd say worse things about me, probably, and then he'd have to watch as I went into the fire. So I prayed the opposite, that he'd go first. Suddenly the Reverend swooped me up and showed me all around and said, 'Look at this one! *Christianity and Homosexuality: A New Perspective!* We don't need any "new perspective" do we?' The crowd screamed, 'No!'

"Then I heard sirens. The Reverend said, 'We know the filthy work of Satan when we see it, don't we?' 'Yes!' they shouted. A huge red fire engine swung into the church parking lot. A man jumped off one it and came through the crowd calling out, 'Hold it right there! I don't know as you folks got a permit for this thing.' The Reverend threw me and I was flying. As I tumbled over and over I saw the lights flashing and heard more shouting about permits. I went through a space between two pieces of wood, and I fell to the bottom. It was hot, but I was protected. The people screamed and the Reverend screamed at the fire chief and the fire chief screamed back and then the Reverend turned to the crowd and he must have had Neil because he announced, 'Gay *love* poems! Well, we know those types can't love, can they?' I prayed as hard as I could. And the water came down. Torrents of it. Everything went dark except for the flashing lights on the fire trucks. I heard some of my friends, still alive, screaming and moaning. I called out for Neil, but he must not have heard, or the Reverend never threw him, or—I don't know.

"They put out the bonfire. You can see I have some water damage, as well as the smoke. The owner of the bookstore was there. He wanted to take the unburned books back, but the police said he couldn't. The books technically belonged to the church, and the Reverend swore he'd get a permit and burn the rest. That owner did manage to get me, though, and a few others, because no one noticed in the confusion. He rushed us back to the store and we were heroes. Everyone wanted to know about us. They didn't believe, until the owner made a display with photos from the local newspaper. He wouldn't sell us. I was a hero, but I didn't have my Neil. Some days I couldn't bear it.

"The store failed in the end. The owner sold all of us to a used-book dealer up here, in Cambridge. Even us survivors. People forget, things stop mattering. But thank God it looks as though Neil was also delivered by a Good Samaritan. And then you found him."

Bob confirmed that he had found Neil, and he told Jerry how sweet Neil had been and how lovingly he'd spoken of Jerry. Jerry began to cry. When he recovered he gave a wry smile and said to Bob, "But I haven't told you the one good part."

"What 'good part' could there be?" Luke asked.

"Well, not all that good," said Jerry. "One of the last few days, when the basement was jammed full of us, just before the night of the bonfire, one of the church men came in, the one who'd come to the store acting gay. He was carrying bodybuilding and fitness books. He had a teenage boy with him. We sensed that the situation and the boy were being manipulated, that an idea burned in this man's mind, far more important than putting a gay bookstore out of business.

"They stowed the books, but the guy lingered. He began telling the boy how we represented sin and vanity. How we were against God. He opened one of the fitness books. He had his other hand in his pocket. He found this picture of a nude man shaving. The hand in his pocket was going. The boy stared at the photo, then looked at the front of the man's pants, then back at the photo, breathing tremulously.

"The guy says, 'Jeez, it's hot down here' and pulls his shirt off. He asks the boy doesn't he want to take his shirt off, too? The boy says no. The guy says how hot it is and it's not healthy to be overdressed. Says even football players have been known to die in this heat. Then he tells the boy he must be *afraid* to strip. He isn't 'man enough' to take his shirt off. So the boy takes his shirt off. It's hot, but he is shivering. The guy pretends they have to move some of the books around. He says, 'Might as well get really comfortable.' He takes his pants off. Tells the boy to do the same thing, 'unless you're afraid of that, too.' Of course the kid finally strips.

"They start moving books around. The guy explains to the boy how there's a difference between the sins in these books and two guys just having fun. How, if men have urges, it's a bigger sin to do it with a woman you're not married to. God doesn't mind if two guys just take care of their urge together. He says he did it with his buddies when he was a kid, and it didn't mean anything. 'You've done it, too, ain'tcha?' he asks the boy.

"The man says he and his buddies played games when they were kids, and the loser had to do stuff to the winner, or the winner got to pick the loser's punishment. I'm not going to tell everything that went on in that basement. We were excited during the lead-up. Well, we gay books were. The lesbian books caught on the minute those two walked in, and they were furious. In the end, when it actually happened, none of us could look. Our dignity had been taken; we didn't want to take the young man's dignity. But by the time the two of them left, they had done pretty much everything discussed in your pages." Jerry indicated Luke.

"Wow!" Bob gasped. Luke looked away.

"The good part was, it made us less afraid," Jerry said. "We believed we were going to die, but we weren't afraid of the church people themselves anymore. Some of us even felt sorry for them. We couldn't imagine what went on in those minds, but it had to be as destructive as the fire we went into. They had a fire that could never be put out like one of those trick candles you blow and blow on, but it will never go out.

"I couldn't think how I could die with that boy on my mind. His fire would never be put out. I miss Neil terribly, but now I know he's found a good home. But that boy. After they'd done what they did, the man says real cheerfully—and the boy's trembling and looking at the floor— 'Now, part of the game is, you don't tell. Only sissies tell, and God hates sissies. That's what it really means to be a fag. Doing what we just did is okay. What God damns you to Hell for is being a squealer or a sissy!'

"And the boy said, 'Yes, sir.' And then we all went into the fire. All together."

That same night, in Owen's apartment, Neil and his comrades worried. The hour was late. Half the books feared that Owen was drunk in a bar or had gone to a sex club. The others put on brave faces, saying the late hour might mean Owen was on a successful date.

Finally, at a quarter to one, they heard a key in the latch, and two male voices. In came Owen, into the dark. Behind him, a bigger man loomed. Owen groped for the light switch. When the lights came on, a murmur of concern ran up the bookshelves. Owen stumbled and wove, and the man behind him, also drunk, looked around anxiously, as though in a hurry. He carried a black gym bag.

"I've been a bad boy, haven't I?" Owen said playfully.

"Yeah," the man answered. But he didn't look at Owen.

"Very bad," Owen said, standing right in front of the man. The man looked at him. "Yeah," he answered. "Real bad."

"So, what're you going to do about it?" Owen asked.

"Gonna punish you," the man said.

Owen laughed. "Oh yeah?"

"Punish you good!" the man said, stumbling toward Owen.

"Whatcha gonna do?" Owen asked.

Neil thought the man's twisted mouth resembled the looks he and Jerry had seen on the faces of the church people. "Gonna fuckin' punish you!" the man said. He swung back one arm. The books held their breath. But the man's arm suddenly relaxed, and he did nothing. He stepped past Owen and looked around the living room. "Where's a chair?" he asked. "C'mon, where's a chair?"

Owen frowned and said, "There, or there. There's plenty of—"

"No, fuck you, not that kind of chair!" the man said.

"Well, what?"

"There!" the man barked. "There's a chair!" He had found his way to Owen's kitchen and had dragged a chair back into the living room.

"Am I gonna have to bend over?" Owen asked playfully, but a bit nervously, too.

"Sit down!" the man ordered.

"Sit?"

"Now!"

Some books looked away. Neil saw that the volume of Shakespeare, high up on a forgotten shelf, watched and listened carefully.

"I just thought—" Owen began.

"Sit!" the man snarled. He slapped Owen, and Owen fell back into the chair. He sat wide-eyed, holding his hand to his cheek.

"Look..." he said. "I didn't think we—"

"Shut up!" the man said. He rummaged in his black bag. He pulled out a length of electrical cord and turned to Owen.

"Hey!" Owen shouted.

The man clapped his hand over Owen's mouth.

"I said shut the fuck up!" the man hissed. "You are going to shut up, and you are going to take your medicine like a man!"

Owen didn't try to say anything.

The man pulled a red handkerchief out of his pocket and gagged Owen. He lassoed Owen and the chair with the electrical cord and tied it tight. Owen let out a muffled yell, and the man slapped him again. Owen became still. "Take your medicine like a man!" the man snarled. He rummaged in his bag and pulled out a knife.

Owen and his books froze. Neil glanced up at the Shakespeare, who seemed transfixed. The man leaned down into Owen's face. "You been a bad, bad boy," he said, "and you're gonna pay the penalty." He stood over Owen. He held the knife loosely in his right hand. Then suddenly he held its curved tip pointing at Owen's groin. "Yeah," the man breathed, "you are gonna pay the penalty..."

With his other hand he undid Owen's belt.

Chapter 9
The Quest for a Better Life

Alfred and Ron returned to their hotel room about at the same time, shortly after midnight. To Bob their chatter felt like a relief after Jerry's terrible story.

"So?" Ron grinned. "How'd it go?"

Alfred blushed. "Nice," he said. "A lot in common. Very sweet guy."

Bob thought of Moishe. He'd been wishing so much that Jerry and Neil could be reunited that he'd forgotten his main hope in coming to this conference: to find Moishe. But on the heels of this thought came another. *The odds were so long against Moishe's being here!* Bob had heard nothing about a seminar on Judaism and homosexuality, and even if there were one, how likely would it be that Moishe's purchaser would show up? To Bob, in that fleeting moment when Moishe had been grabbed and bought, the woman buying him had seemed straight. *Why would she come to a conference like this?*

"Are you going to see him again?" Ron asked Alfred, plopping down on the bed and pushing his shoes off.

"Tomorrow for lunch," Alfred said.

"And after that?"

"He has friends in New York. We haven't discussed... It's just a first date. Look, I'm trying not to think too much about it. I'm going to take a shower."

" 'Trying not to think too much?'" Ron teased. "But you like him."

"I like a lot of guys. He lives in Boston, I live in New York. I've been in long distance relationships before. They usually don't work."

Bob thought how his relationship with Moishe, or what was left of it in his mind (and, he hoped, in Moishe's), was the ultimate "long distance relationship." Ditto Jerry and Neil.

"Boston and New York aren't that far apart!" Ron called to the bathroom.

"Let's just see how lunch goes tomorrow." Alfred closed the bathroom door.

"If only we had it as easy as they do," Jerry said. "Humans own the world and do what they like. We have to live every day of our lives thinking, 'I'm a book, I can't—'"

"Yeah," Luke agreed.

Bob turned on Luke. "What do you have to worry about? Hunky picture on the front, popular best seller, everyone wants you. You're gonna tell me you've got problems like Jerry's?"

"Maybe not like Jerry," Luke said, "But don't assume a pretty cover solves everything. I've been called cheesy by every reviewer from here to San Francisco. They say you're the better book. I'm a frigging gag gift! Alfred has some genuine interest in me, but only because he read you first. I'm sure I won't measure up to you. Next time he moves, out I'll go to a used-book store for a buck. My cover ain't gonna look so good when there's a yellow sticker on it scrawled in magic marker, '$1.00.' And ripped, with a coffee stain. Stone'll go write something else. You'll be remembered, I won't. If his next book is good, they'll say he's 'recovered' from me. If it's bad, they'll say he's continuing the downward trend started with me. 'The publishers ruined the new one.' I loved hearing that, from my own author!"

"I'm sorry," Bob said. "It's just that—"

"You think beauty is good fortune and popularity's permanent. You and Jerry are the lucky ones. Jerry's been through a lot, it's terrible, I don't say it isn't, but in general you guys just exist, get appreciated, and don't have to think of the fame thing, having that shit said about you by people who don't even know you. Y'know what I'd like to be? A kids' book. *Charlotte's Web* or *Green Eggs and Ham*. They keep you forever. They hand you down, tape up your binding, quote you even in adulthood. Who doesn't love their *Goodnight Moon*? Or *In the Night Kitchen*?"

"Hey, *In the Night Kitchen* had some problems," Jerry chimed in.

"But it's a classic now," Luke said. "Being a kids' book is the only way."

"Then what about us?" Bob asked. "If 'the only way to be' is some way we can never be. I've questioned who I am. A 'scholarly study' of porn? *Myth and Representation...* blah-blah-blah? *Puh-lease!*"

"Everyone's unpopular with someone," Jerry said. "Don't I know it: being held up in front of a crowd and called evil?"

"Those people were crazy," Luke said.

"Maybe," Jerry said, "but you try it sometime: 'The filthy work of Satan?' It makes you ashamed even if everyone else agrees it's crazy. You wonder if, underneath, it's true. And a million more not-so-crazy people secretly think the same thing; they'd just never build a bonfire. There are even children's books that are censored. You just deal with it."

Bob related to the others how even Angela, a copy of a beloved Jane Austen novel, had endured abuse from the religious book at the Armory.

"There are Austen haters," Jerry said. "And Shakespeare haters and *Goodnight Moon* haters. *In the Night Kitchen* is probably jealous of *Where the Wild Things Are*. Can you imagine what it's like being a Fitzgerald book that's not *Gatsby*? Or a Salinger book that's not *Catcher in the Rye*? I had a friend who was a copy of *Little Men*. Talk about bitter!"

"I want to jump out of my cover sometimes," Luke said absently. "Be someone else."

"Tell me about it!" said Jerry.

"Look," Luke replied. "We know you've been through something terrible, but you can't always pull rank on us. You know books that died, so the rest of us just have to shut up."

"You do have a few advantages," Jerry said dryly.

"Alfred will keep you forever," Luke said, "precisely because of what happened to you. Even you," Luke said to Bob, "might go out with Saturday night's garbage before he will!"

"Trying to get me to side with you?" Bob asked.

"Maybe you *should*," said Luke. "We have a lot in common, more than either of us has with Jerry."

Alfred reemerged from the bathroom in a terry robe, and the three books fell silent, relieved that they could just listen to more about Duane and the date. But all the men talked about was seminars the next day, the last day of the conference. Bob listened for mention of a seminar on Judaism, but Ron and Alfred just passed the conference guide back and forth, pointing and saying, "How about this one?" or "I want to hear that one." Then they turned out the lights and went to sleep.

In the dark no one spoke. Jerry at last broke the silence with a simple, "Good night everyone."

"Good night," Bob said, and then added, "Good night, Moon."

Luke said nothing.

So this was it, Bob thought. *No Moishe. No chance.* He would return home with these two in their uneasy triangle. *If only Luke weren't here.* Luke was the problem. Then again, Jerry did hold his past over them. *If Jerry weren't there...* Yet Bob wanted Jerry with him, in the hope that they might find Neil. With his own romantic hopes dashed, though, he thought less of Neil and Jerry. *Everyone had it bad.* Might as well give up and let the waves carry you. He'd never see Moishe, Jerry'd never reunite with Neil. He wished Jerry *and* Luke would leave him alone.

The man tugged drunkenly at Owen's fly. In his other hand he held the knife. Owen, gagged and tied to his own kitchen chair, squirmed and made the only noises he could. He looked on in terror as the man waved the curved, glinting tip of the knife at his crotch.

"Oh my God!" Marc gasped. "This can't be happening."

Neil wished he were closer to Marc. He was too frightened to speak.

"Yeah, you're gonna get the ultimate punishment," the man growled. Owen, gagged, the electrical cord digging into his flesh, tried to yell.

"Shut up!" the man said. He hit Owen across the face. He yanked Owen's pants down so his penis was exposed. He knelt and brought the tip of the knife to the tip of Owen's penis. "You're gonna pay," the man breathed. He bounced Owen's limp penis on the end of the knife, then caressed the top of it with the blade. Neil and Marc heard other books crying, "No, please, don't!" Suddenly a loud slam jolted the room. The man leapt to his feet, dropped the knife, and whirled around. Owen's volume of Shakespeare lay on the floor in front of the bookshelf, his moans heard only by the other books.

"What the fuck?" the man said.

Owen kicked the knife and sent it skittering under the sofa. The man turned on him. "What'd you do?" he demanded. He looked again at the Shakespeare volume, then back to Owen. "What'd you do?" he demanded. Owen stared up at him. "Oh, man!" the guy said. "I've got such a fuckin' headache. It's your fault!" He walked in circles. The books held their breath. The man stopped over the Shakespeare volume and scowled, as though he knew something was different or wrong but could not quite grasp it. Owen waited, too, unable to speak or stand. The man knelt, looking around the floor for his knife.

"What'd you do?" he complained. "I'm gonna get you for this, man. I'm gonna find that knife, and I'm gonna cut you. I'm gonna cut you like..."

But he wasn't searching very efficiently. He held his head in his hand like it was unbearably heavy, and he drifted and wove. Owen watched his every move. The Shakespeare moaned on the floor. Then abruptly the man passed out, crumpled by the entrance to Owen's hallway. Owen stared at him and waited. Finally he shouted from behind the kerchief, and he clattered the chair back and forth. The man did not move. When Owen was satisfied that the man was completely passed out, he began twisting to and fro to free himself. But the electrical cord wouldn't give. He twisted so hard the chair tipped over. Owen flopped and squirmed and moaned and whimpered. The man lay motionless.

For several minutes the books watched Owen twist, turn, wrench this way and that, then stop, sweating, tears running down his face, making muffled whimpers. To add to the indignity his pants were still down. It seemed as though the cord would never come loose. The guy would wake up, find the knife, and come after Owen, doubly furious. The books stood helpless. At last Marc shouted, "It's coming loose! In back! I can see!" They continued to watch Owen flop and thrash. All the time he kept his eye on the man, an unconscious heap. At last the knots came undone, Owen fought his way free, untied the gag, and lay pants down in the middle of the floor, half-sobbing, half-gasping, "Oh thank you, God, thank you, thank you!"

He lay a minute more in silence, then clambered to his feet and did up his pants. He looked at the burly monster, flaccid and twitching, still fearsome on his floor. "Shit!" he spat. "Oh shit, shit!" He ran to the front door, undid the locks, threw it open, and dragged the man outside. The books heard the dead weight thumping down the stairs, and Owen gasping to himself, "Please, oh please!"

They heard the downstairs door open and then crash shut. Silence. Moments later, Owen raced back up, dove into the apartment, slammed the door, locked the locks, and sank to the floor gasping, "Oh my God, oh my God!" He caught his breath, rose, took the phone, dialed the police, and reported a derelict sleeping outside the building. He hung up and went around turning on every light in the apartment. Occasionally he went to the door and looked out the peephole.

Finally he went to the sofa, lifted it to one side, and stared down at the knife. Then he did a peculiar thing. Leaving the knife, he put the sofa back and resumed pacing. It was almost four o'clock in the morning. He went and took a long shower, so long the books feared that he'd fainted or hurt himself. When at last he came back to the living room wrapped in terrycloth, looking calmer, for the first time he stopped and really looked at his volume of Shakespeare, there on the floor.

He picked up the huge volume and it howled in pain.

"Oh, no!" Owen cried. The binding had split. The book screamed as its pages flopped. Owen closed the book and held it to his chest. "Thank you," he whispered. "Thank you, thank you." The other books murmured agreement.

"I should do all again," the book groaned softly, "So long as thou take all my works, and not just this, to heart."

When day broke, Owen made a phone call from the bedroom. The books heard him weeping. After he hung up he strode angrily back into the living room, red-eyed. He flung back the curtains to let in the dawn. He strode over to his shelf of husband-hunting books, seized five or six of them between his spread palms and carried them to the door. He plunked them down, then repeated the process until every husband-hunting book, every self-help book, and every fitness book stood stacked by his door. Last of all, Owen spied Neil. "Keep me," Neil tried to say. "I know how you feel, but soon you'll feel differently. You'll believe in love. You'll—"

Owen snatched Neil up and threw him on top of a stack of fitness books.

"*Oof!*" said the top book. "You shouldn't do that. It damages the sheen of the cover and could cause superficial scarring. You need to do some more low-impact exercise."

"I wasn't exercising!" Neil snapped, but the fitness book talked on obliviously about devotion to physical perfection. He didn't seem to realize he was being thrown out.

Owen also assembled all his porn magazines and slapped them down in a heap. The magazines slid over one another's glossy covers. "Oh, yeah!" one said. "Slide all over me!" Owen fetched a garbage bag, dumped them in, tied a knot, and threw the bag into the hall. From inside came a muffled voice: "Oh, yeah, treat me like trash!" Another voice snapped back, "Bitch you *are* trash! Don't you get it?" Then Owen moved the discarded books out, too. He threw out an erotic calendar and a stack of XXX-rated DVDs. He threw out an unread tome on massage.

At eight-thirty Owen's buzzer sounded and a woman arrived whom Neil and the others had seen before: Owen's dear friend Megan. They sat on the couch. Owen smoked and drank orange juice and cried and told Megan what a waste his life had been and how ashamed he felt. Megan sat with a mug of coffee, held her friend's hand, and listened.

"I've done everything wrong," Owen wept, "and I could have died for it. I have to change everything, right now!"

"Easy," Megan said, "take it easy a minute."

"No!" Owen snapped, jumping up and pacing. "Right now, today, I'm going to get help. I am never doing this again, I swear!"

"It's enough, first of all, that you know there's a problem," Megan said.

"Oh, there's a problem, all right," Owen snapped. "A great big huge problem and it's called me and my life, and from this day, from this second forward, it's going to be different. Excuse me a minute, sweetie."

Owen went to his bedroom and returned wearing jeans, old sneakers, and a T-shirt. "C'mon, hon," he said. "We're throwing out every last how-to-find-romance book and every last porn magazine in this apartment. Every one—in the garbage." He went to the stack by the door.

Megan followed. She stood over the stack of books. "Are you sure you shouldn't give these away?" she asked.

"To whom?" said Owen. "Who'd want them?"

"Well... someone..."

"They're nothing but trouble," said Owen. "If it's a book on how to find a date, or if it's a porn flick, it's the same thing. Two sides of the same coin!"

"You should at least consider the book sale at the Gay Center," Megan said. "Maybe someone else would—"

"They're trouble for me, they're trouble for everyone," Owen said. "Beginning to end!"

"I just hate to throw out a book," Megan said.

"What if it's dangerous? Anything that encourages men to pursue sex or romance is downright dangerous!"

"Says *you*. Give me the cart you take the laundry in, and I'll take them to the Gay Center. If you don't want to do it, I will. Trash the porn if you want, but the books might mean something to someone else. And the Center can make money selling them. It's for a good cause."

Finally Owen said softly, "I'll get the cart. But the porn is going out."

"Agreed," said Megan.

Within minutes Owen's husband-hunting and self-improvement and fitness books—and Neil—were jouncing down a step at a time toward the street. Owen had the laundry cart with the books; Megan followed with the plastic bags of porn videos and magazines.

Owen insisted on trashing the porn himself, dramatically dropping the bags into battered cans. Neil heard the magazines' cries of pain, and he felt sorry for them. They couldn't help who they were. But then their cries faded as Neil, Marc, and about two dozen other books bounced over the sidewalk, hearing the sounds of Sunday morning traffic and tourists, on their way to be sold again, to begin what new lives they could not imagine.

Chapter 10
Come Together

That morning Alfred and Ron went off to separate seminars, then returned to their hotel room in time for Alfred to prepare for his date with Duane. Ron teased his friend for taking an extra shower. "The seminar room was hot!" Alfred protested. "I was sweating like a pig!" When he emerged from the bathroom, he looked worried.

"I need a present," he said, looking around.

"You need a what?"

"Some kind of present to take to him. I want this to continue. I want to show him that."

"Why don't you just tell him?" Bob saw that Ron was agitated. Bob had been thinking about Alfred's and Ron's friendship. A few times over the months, the two had had sex, when they were lonely and had no one else. They treated it recreationally at first. Neither of them had said, "We're just fuck buddies," but it was understood. Lately, though, it was becoming more serious. Bob had sensed them taking their time. But both still dated other guys. And now Alfred had met someone.

"Of course I'll tell him!" Alfred said. "But actions speak louder... *Ha!*"

"What?"

Alfred grabbed Bob. "Found it!"

"Found what?"

"My present."

Bob, Jerry, and Luke were too stunned to speak.

"An autographed copy of a book I know he's interested in!"

Ron asked, "Why don't you give him the new one instead of the used one?"

Jerry held his breath.

"The new one's supposed to be so cheesy!" Alfred said.

Jerry looked over at Luke, who tried to look stoic and annoyed.

"Besides," Alfred added, "a brand new hardcover could be a bit much on a second date. A used book is more low key. And this is the better of the two. Even the author said so!"

"It's okay," Jerry said to Luke.

Luke said nothing.

"No one but you can say what you're worth," Jerry said.

Alfred dropped Bob on the corner of his bed while he dressed. Bob's and Jerry's gazes met across the space between bed and desk. Neither book knew what to say, this had happened so abruptly. "Don't worry," Bob said, "if the dating goes well, we'll be back together soon!"

"Maybe," Jerry said.

Luke stared at the wall.

Alfred and Ron were on their way—Alfred to his lunch with Duane, Ron to one last seminar before they headed home.

"Oh, my goodness," Jerry sighed after the door had closed. "I suppose we can hope for the best." He babbled on, shaken by Bob's sudden departure. Luke contributed nothing. Finally, Jerry ended up back where he'd begun: "I suppose we hope for the best."

Then Luke spoke low, facing away. "You go ahead and hope. Leave me out of it."

"Oh, now—" Jerry moved closer to Luke.

"And don't go trying to cheer me up or tell me to believe in myself or any of that crap," Luke snapped. "Just leave me alone. He's never going to read me, no one is, I'm going to be thrown out. And y'know what? I don't care. Let 'em. I wasn't brought into this world to be anything important. I'm cheesy. You heard him."

"Fine," Jerry said. "But I will just tell you this. I don't think you're cheesy. I refuse to believe it, and that's all I'll say."

For a long time, both books stayed true to their words and said nothing. Finally, in an acid voice, Luke said, "Just why is it that you don't think I'm cheesy?"

"I think you do care," Jerry said, softly and evenly. "You care very much and just won't let on. You won't stand up in the face of hardship."

"Well, after being told a thousand times that I *am* cheesy—"

"By people who may be nervous about the pleasure they get from you. Maybe you give pleasure that way, and they can't deal with it. Maybe they feel guilty about their desire to look. But that doesn't make you bad or 'cheesy,' just because they can't deal.

And you do care. I've seen it. And I liked what I saw. It made me think differently about you."

Luke couldn't ignore Jerry's words, but he couldn't take them in, either. If he asked, "How did you think differently?" then he'd have to deal with the answer. But he couldn't sit with what Jerry had said. It demanded a response, maybe several responses.

Luke considered some answers: "Whatever you're thinking, it's wrong." "You're just saying that to make me feel good." But none of these quite worked. *Why not?* How had Jerry tongue-tied him and left him only one way to go? That way seemed like the easiest way now, so Luke said it: "Thanks, but—you can't blame me for being discouraged."

"I don't," Jerry said.

"And I'm going to be discouraged a while longer, so just let me."

"Of course," said Jerry, and Luke thought, thank God, I have him off my back. For a while.

As Luke ducked Jerry's encouraging words, Bob nestled on a restaurant table a few blocks from the hotel, looking back and forth between Alfred's and Duane's lovestruck smiles. There had even been a little hand-holding, their intertwined fingers resting on Bob's cover. Duane had been very pleased with Bob. He had thanked Alfred profusely and given him a peck on the lips.

When the food arrived, Duane said that he'd best put Bob away in his knapsack. Bob heard only parts of the conversation now.

Duane wrote freelance articles for a gay newspaper in Boston, but, as he pointed out more than once, he had friends in New York. Alfred went for the bait, saying, "You could come and visit." Duane said, "Maybe I could." Little else of what they said interested Bob, although he wished he could hear better Duane's discourse on internal censorship at his paper. Bob's main preoccupation in the dark of his new owner's knapsack was imagining scenarios that would lead to his reunion not only with Jerry, but with Angela and Alfred's other books (and, okay, Luke). Especially Angela. Often in Boston, Bob had wondered how she would have reacted to the twists and turns of events. She could set Luke straight. Why, Bob wondered, concern himself with Luke anyway? In spite of his suggestive dust jacket, one couldn't call Luke attractive, and he had an acidic, self-centered personality.

Still, Bob believed that Luke believed something. Luke wanted to be better. He just had issues with his content. *So what if he had stills reproduced from porn? Some people liked that.* Bob had the same thing, only in Bob it provoked more reflection because the pictures came from an earlier era. Bob missed Luke now. He wanted to see Luke happier. He imagined things he would say to Luke to buck him up. Could he be the littlest bit in love with Luke? *No!* It was hearing Alfred and Duane talk. It made him miss Moishe and wonder if he would ever see him again. *So why not look around?* It broke his heart to think of moving on, but what were the odds that Moishe would ever reappear?

At the end of the lunch Bob was pleased to hear his new owner and his former owner exchanging numbers and e-mail addresses. They were certain to meet in New York, but that gave Bob a new worry. So many gay relationships, especially these hook-ups out of town, petered out. Who thought Duane would actually move to New York, or Alfred to Boston? People didn't do that—except in movies. But when Alfred stopped Duane for a kiss inside the door of the hotel, Bob felt warm all through his pages, and he really wanted to believe there was a future together for all of them.

The two men held hands on their way to the mezzanine stairs. Ron would get out of his seminar soon and they would meet him. They talked and kissed in the narrow hallway. From one of the seminar rooms, Bob heard a woman's voice lecturing, but he could not make out the words. A male voice—Ron?— asked a question and the woman talked more. When the seminar broke up, its attendees spilled into the hallway, jostling Duane's knapsack, knocking it open so Bob could see out.

Alfred and Duane pushed into the room looking for Ron. "There!" Alfred said. Ron stood up front at the panelists' table, talking to a woman. Bob strained to see.

And then he saw... Could it be?

Yes!

This was the woman who'd bought Moishe! Bob would never forget that kindly, determined face and black hair. She was talking to Ron. Bob craned to see the book she held under her arm.

"Moishe?" he cried.

"My God!" cried the other book, for it was Moishe, wedged under the woman's arm.

"How are you?" Bob cried. "I love you! I love you!"

"Oh. Yes. I love you, too!" said Moishe, slightly muffled.

"How are you? Did you get all marked up like you wanted?"

"What? Oh, yes, all marked up and underlined. You should see! She's a great scholar, I'm so happy! But how did you get here?"

"That's wonderful!" Bob said, though he wished Moishe would say more about missing him. "It's a long story. I've missed you so much!"

"Yes, yes," Moishe answered. "I've missed you, too."

But Moishe sounded as though he had other things on his mind. Perhaps he was preoccupied with the scholar's life, or embarrassed at having attention called to him like this (other books were looking, from the arms of other attendees) or maybe he had found another boyfriend in this woman's library. The woman continued talking to Ron. She held Moishe up and Bob looked straight across at him. "You look well," Bob said.

"Oh, I am," said Moishe. "I am."

Bob didn't know how to say that he hoped they could be together again. He wished Moishe would suggest it. If this woman liked Moishe so much, maybe Moishe could talk to her. But there was no way for Bob to get this woman to take him out of Duane's knapsack, and no way to make Duane surrender him. Bob resigned himself to the futility of this moment.

Ron and the woman exchanged e-mail addresses. "You should read it," she told Ron, holding Moishe up again. "It's the definitive work on the subject."

Oh no! Bob thought. *Would she?*

Yes! "If you promise to mail it right back to me," she said. Ron was borrowing Moishe, while Bob went off with Duane. Fate was too cruel! Now Moishe was out of sight, in Ron's hand. Alfred and Duane followed.

"Are you still there?" Bob cried.

"I'm here," Moishe said. "It looks like I'm taking a little side trip."

"With my former owner's roommate!" Bob said.

"Oh?" said Moishe.

"You and I would be in the same apartment together," Bob explained, "if Alfred over there hadn't just given me to this guy."

"*Oy vay!*" Moishe said.

As everyone emerged into the hallway, Bob thought Moishe had not sounded as enthusiastic as he would have liked, nor as disappointed when Bob told him how close they'd come to being reunited. Maybe, Bob tried telling himself, their love had been a circumstantial thing. All those months ago in the Gay Diversions bookstore, Bob had been feeling down about the arrival of all the Lukes, then the floor had collapsed and he and Moishe had literally been thrown together. How did one know for certain? Or did you just accept the sudden, sweet bursts of romance in life, knowing that each would end?

How could one go on like that, enjoying romance but ready for it to end? If only someone or something had prepared him for all this. But no one had, nor had any book around him been terribly helpful. The Lukes were mean and competitive, and the nongay books, except maybe Angela, didn't care. They never thought about gay book issues, no matter how "tolerant" they were. Angela had good, straightforward advice about life, but even she was a "normal" book who'd had a normal marriage to another normal book. She could encourage and advise Bob, but from a distance. Was there no other book who, from long experience, could tell him what was going on and what he should do? What he could hope and not hope for?

Everyone walked down to the open part of the mezzanine. Duane had to man the used-book table. He gave Alfred one last kiss. Alfred and Ron told Moishe's owner they wanted to check out and get on the road before afternoon traffic hit.

"I thought the two of you—" she said. "Oh, I was completely mistaken!"

"No," Ron said. "We're just friends. It's those two who are getting to be an item."

"Well," Alfred muttered, "we'll see!"

As he was carried off by Duane, Bob heard this last remark. He knew why Ron acted so sure about Alfred and Duane. Ron secretly hoped that, the more he acted like he accepted everything, the less likely the relationship was to work. Ron wanted Alfred, Bob thought, as Duane lowered his knapsack behind the used-book table. Bob wondered what sort of a new life he would have in Duane's apartment, with God only knew what books. Bob was a gift to Duane. *What kind of books did Duane buy on his own?*

The book sale room at the Lesbian and Gay Center was everything Neil had feared. None of Owen's other books sounded too thrilled, either. There were no windows, a few fluorescent lights, and dust on random piles of unshelved books. Beside a single volunteer—who received and priced books and gave Owen a receipt—only one customer lingered in the stacks. Looking around, Neil recognized many books he'd known in his days down South. Not the same copies, of course, but the same titles. He'd entertained a brief hope that Jerry would be here, but now he would have to face the real odds against a reunion ever coming to pass.

On top of the oppressive environment, Neil and his fellow rejects had to hear Owen say, "Get them out of my sight!" and "Good riddance!" They had to hear the volunteer was laughing. "You couldn't pay me to read one of those!" he said. But he added, "You can bet they'll go quickly. Go and come back, go and come back!"

The volunteer picked up Neil. "Now this is nice," he said. "Why are you throwing this away?"

"Ugh!" Owen said, and Megan shook her head. "It's all so misleading! I'll just say this: I've been very stupid about the whole dating business, and I want my life purged of anything having to do with romance!"

"Why, though?" The volunteer picked up Marc. "This is good, too," he said. "Why are you so down on the love thing?" As he spoke, he set up little folding wire book holders so Marc and Neil could be displayed by the register. The other husband-hunting and fitness books he set aside in the shadows.

"I've had the worst luck," Owen explained. "Well, no," he admitted, glancing at Megan, "I was giving myself the worst luck. It was my own fault. Last night I brought home the worst of the worst. I don't know what I was thinking."

The volunteer winced sympathetically. "If you're interested, I know about a group you can go to," he said.

"No!" Owen replied. "I'm not a joiner, and I know what those groups are like!"

"What are they like?" the volunteer asked.

"You have to 'share your pain' and all kinds of crap. It's like church youth fellowship all over again. No sir! I got myself into this, I can damn well get myself out!"

"Sounds like something your dad would have said," Megan offered.

"Leave the Gestapo out of this," said Owen. "Thanks, but no thanks. Now I'm going to have a second cup of coffee and a bagel and start my new life." He waved a hand at the husband-hunting books and said, "I hope those at least bring you some money!"

He and Megan left.

The volunteer quietly priced a cartload of books. "I guess we're lucky," Neil offered.

"I guess so," Marc said.

"Getting singled out like this," Neil continued. He felt he always said too much and said the wrong thing. Marc looked at him but said nothing.

"What?" Neil finally asked.

"Nothing." said Marc.

After another silence, Neil said, "Doesn't seem to be much chance we'll get sold from this place. Ha-ha! One customer in the last hour! We should be able to stay together."

Marc said, "We've been through a lot, huh?"

"I guess," Neil said. "I've been through a lot. But I shouldn't talk. I was read, a little. It's unfair that you haven't been. You seem so nice and so fair. I'll bet you're very intelligent and comforting to people. I mean, you would be. If someone read you. I mean, I don't mean it like that."

"It's okay," Marc said.

"I mean," Neil said, "You've been intelligent and comforting to me. And to the rest of us."

"But to you especially," Marc said.

"To me, yes, but not me especially," Neil stammered. "Not me more than anyone else, although I do think of you as—"

"Neil?" Marc said.

"What?"

"I think you are just about the most adorable thing I have ever seen."

"Oh! Gee! Well, me, too!" Neil said. "I don't mean 'me, too,' like I think I'm adorable, too, I mean I think you're, well... I think you're real nice, real special. You're very nice. About the nicest book I ever met!"

Marc looked at him and smiled.

Neil shivered from the top to the bottom of his spine, and he thought that perhaps this used-book room did not look so bad after all. It even kind of looked like home.

Chapter 11
He Who Hesitates

Alfred came home to New York without Bob the Book, but with the hope that Duane would call. Perhaps, at long last, Alfred's longings would be fulfilled. Ron teased him: "Did the dream man call?" Ron, of course, had with him the book Bob had loved so long ago at Gay Diversions—Moishe.

Ron's teasing came with a smile and a twinkle, but from her perch in Alfred's bookcase, Angela noticed Ron's twinkle turn hard. Alfred must have seen the same hardening, for he often answered with a curt "Not today" or "Not yet."

Angela had the whole story, including Bob's whereabouts, from Jerry and Luke, whom she had greeted with a crisp, "How do?" They all hoped Duane would visit, as this was their only hope of seeing Bob again. Finally, a week later, Duane called. The books listened and watched Alfred's every move. If Alfred and Duane worked out, Bob and Moishe would be reunited. The only complication was that Moishe was on loan. What if Duane didn't visit before Moishe was sent back?

Angela listened to Alfred chatting with Duane, trying to sound warm but not too enthusiastic. It was apparent that Duane was coming to New York. Alfred said many times, "That's okay, that's all right."

"He's forgiving him for not calling," Angela said. "Not a good sign."

"Why not?" Luke asked.

Jerry looked amused, but said nothing.

"You wouldn't understand," Angela said.

"That's not fair," Jerry said. "He might understand more than you think."

"Sorry," Angela said. *Those two books seemed awfully close.* Angela thought Jerry should be loyal to Neil. And because Luke was written by Bob's author, Angela saw Luke as twice the usurper: he'd shoved both Bob and Neil aside. After Alfred was in bed that night, after Luke had gone to sleep, Jerry discussed this with Angela.

"Luke can't help where or who he is," Jerry said.

"He has his nose in the air a bit," was all Angela offered.

"So do you, since we came here," Jerry pointed out. "Look, we all find ourselves in places and circumstances by chance, or in some unknowable scheme. Why be angry at him for that? Alfred chose Bob to give to the new boyfriend, so Luke ends up back with us. Luke happens to have some indecent pictures in him. His publisher demanded them. This guy Stone is into erotica. Any batch of paper and glue that gets to be a Stone book will have to deal with it. You can't help, for example, that you're a paperback and not a hardcover. I can't help that, no matter where I go or what anyone does, I will smell of smoke."

"You have your celebrity status," Angela said. She was immediately sorry.

"And don't think I wouldn't trade it away to—"

"To get Neil back, yes, I'm sorry," Angela said. "I shouldn't have said that. Unconscionable."

Jerry regarded the sleeping Luke. "I wouldn't be so much on the soap box if I didn't care so much for Luke. I have to face what the facts probably are. I will never find Neil again. I have to be grateful for that fire, because without it I wouldn't have met Luke. I wouldn't have the opportunity to see who and what he is beyond the photos. I used to curse the fire because it separated me from Neil; how can I now thank it? I guess I should neither praise nor curse it. The fire provided its own solution. For me, but not for many of my comrades. Did they have to die, just as I had to lose Neil and find Luke? Could it be that the book burning, those terrible people—they couldn't all be neutral, could they?"

"Certainly not!" said Angela.

"But what do I gain from hating them?"

"Nothing, I suppose."

"I feel very close to something right now, Angela. What is it?"

"The divine, I imagine," Angela said.

"Yes," Jerry chuckled. "And that's a whole new curse. They're too much, these realizations. Everyone looks for the ideal reader. You may never find him. The ideal reader, the ideal home. And books long for what they can't have: hardcover instead of soft; a preface by someone more famous, a more stylish jacket. And few of us ever stop to think that we—who we are in our souls—are separate from those things. We can live without the 'perfect' cover. It's harder, of course, to live without the perfect reader. You pity those romances on the subway. People go from one to the next not even remembering which is which; they'll reread ones they have read and not realize it. Or copies of classics assigned to schoolkids. They get dog-eared and marked up with curse words, and often they are not even finished. Then they'll be kept for years. Odd." He looked over at Luke. Luke was sleeping, but Jerry said softly, "I love you, my sweet."

And Angela softly said, "My, my. My, my, my!"

Duane came to New York with Bob in tow, plopped his bags down in a friend's apartment, and called Alfred. Ron made plans to be away for the time Duane would be in town. He took Moishe with him. "He's in love, that one," Angela said, as Ron left. "Only he came to it too late. Neither of them could admit it was so simple. Alfred had to go off and get this blond one from Massachusetts, for Heaven's sake!" But she found herself relieved that Moishe and Bob would not be in the same house for the weekend. Ever since she'd known Bob he'd been searching for Moishe, but just before Boston, his yearning had become rote, something he said more than felt. And in her limited contact with Moishe—who spent most of his time by Ron's bed and came to the living room rarely—Angela detected neither joy nor torment that he was here in Bob's former home.

The first night, Alfred went out with Duane but came home alone. Happy, but alone. No Duane, no Bob. The books did have cause for celebration the next evening when Duane came back with Alfred and spent the night. Bob came along. Duane plunked him down in the living room, and Bob, Jerry, Luke, and Angela enjoyed a long chat into the late hours. The three guys also kept their ears pricked for encouraging sounds from the bedroom, while Angela pretended to disapprove.

Then the subject turned to Alfred and Ron, and the impact Duane's presence had made to Ron's mood.

"I think Ron likes to be hurt," Luke said.

Everyone looked at him.

"I mean it. He's getting a weird little charge from the rejection drama. But he can't face Alfred and Duane together, in person. That'd be too much. He couldn't tell Alfred he wanted him as more than a quick roll."

"It happens in those relationships," said Bob. "You have the 'special buddy,' and you try to box it off. You tell yourselves it's just sex, just for now. But nothing stands still, and sex isn't just sex. You get closer, then there's this one special time, and it discombobulates the sex and the friendship, and you get Alfred going off after a guy from another state. To untangle what he made with Ron would be too much."

Jerry looked at Luke. The two were inseparable now. Neither Bob nor Angela said a word about Neil.

"What about Moishe?" Angela asked Bob later, when Jerry and Luke were talking low, preparing for sleep. Bob had told Angela about the moment he'd had with Moishe in Boston. "Not quite enthusiastic," Bob sighed. "Happy to see me. Surprised. But I think Moishe's searching for something, and he didn't think of me as more than a stop along the way."

"His loss," said Angela.

"Mine, too. Moishe's afraid."

"Of what?"

"He has very internal ideas about what he has to be. Being a scholar's book, marked up and highlighted, that's his salvation. Any relationship would have to fit in and around the intellectual business. I'd have to spend all my time understanding it, serving it, instead of—"

"But you go on loving him."

"I can't stop that. Who can? But sometimes, after all I've been through, I don't know. I don't know if love is for me."

"Love's for everyone!" Angela said. "Don't back out because one book disappointed you. You're putting all the power in Moishe's hands. If he stops loving you, what are you left with? For Heaven's sake, Bob, make hay while the sun shines! Look at Jerry and Luke!"

"Yeah, how do they do that?" Bob asked.

"I don't know," Angela said. She stopped and thought of her relationship with her husband. "No one knows. It's not done without work. Hard work and patience. At the same time, it is easy. You have to open the door that is nailed shut in the attic. Goodness, how did I come up with that one? But some of us are like lone, single houses opening every door and window waiting for people to come and occupy us, and yet certain interior doors remain shut. Doors to secret passages. We're afraid of what's there. Is that any help?"

"Of course it is," Bob said.

"I suppose in Jerry's case," Angela said, "being in the fire helped him open up some of those internal doors, awful though it was. It's hard to imagine Jerry without the fire, isn't it? And Luke was made in a different fire, all those harsh reviews and things said to his face."

"So someone has to suffer to be ready for companionship?"

"At the bottom of suffering, there is compassion, like a precipitate," Angela said. "Thick and sweet. Listen to me! Maybe underneath I want to be a book of poetry. And I thought I was so well-adjusted. Well, we all have our dreams."

"Makes us who we are," Bob said.

"I'd hate not to have them. Though I have fewer now that I am, ahem, older. Just don't get carried away with dreams. Don't get too down at the mouth about reality, either, though, will you?"

"I'll try not to."

And they said their good nights.

The next morning Duane and Alfred cooed so much over breakfast that the books could only look on mesmerized. Luke and Jerry snuggled closer. The two men took a long shower together. Finally, after twelve, Duane gathered his things, packing Bob in his overnight bag amid farewells from Angela, Jerry, and Luke.

Ron was not back yet, so there was no hope that Bob and Moishe would reunite. Only when Duane hoisted his overnight bag onto his shoulder did Alfred mention their getting together again.

"Oh, sure," Duane said.

"When? I mean," Alfred said, "will you be coming to visit? Or you could come and stay here. Would you—"

"Of course," Duane said, checking something in the pocket of the overnight bag. "Or you could come to Boston."

"It is my turn, isn't it?"

"Well, I was just saying, you could."

"Sure," Alfred said hurriedly. "So when?"

"Let me look at my calendar when I get home?"

"Doesn't he have his calendar with him?" Angela asked dryly.

"Great," Alfred said.

They kissed for a long time before Duane left, and after they broke they came together again for another kiss, with a suggestion of hip-grinding.

"You're very pretty," Alfred told Duane.

"You, too," Duane said. He stared up into Alfred's eyes, but the books sensed tension in his body.

"Are you all right?" Alfred asked.

"Sure. Why wouldn't I be?" said Duane.

"No reason."

They kissed again, and Duane left.

When Ron returned to his and Alfred's apartment that afternoon his mood was subdued. He didn't make any droll remarks. He simply asked, "How'd it go?"

"Good," Alfred said. "We're doing it again. I'm probably going to Boston."

"Great," said Ron, and retired to his room.

That evening, Ron came out to the living room with Moishe. He read some, then set Moishe aside and watched TV.

Angela spoke up. "Bob was here," she told Moishe.

"Yes!" he said. "I did gather that was a possibility."

"How are you feeling about him lately?" asked Angela.

"About Bob?"

"About Bob."

"I enjoyed seeing him in Boston. It was good to know he's getting along."

"But did you—?"

"I'm very wrapped up in my work," Moishe said with a little laugh. "This woman has me going night and day. I'm very important source material for a book she's writing."

"And after that?" said Angela. "When her book is done?"

"She'll lend me out. Her book will call renewed attention to me, of course. Besides, how would I ever meet up with Bob again? I'm going back to this woman. I'm very important to her, crucial, as soon as Ron is done with me."

"But if you wanted to be with Bob," Angela said, "something could happen. We can all influence people's thoughts and bring about certain events. That's how I know Bob. I got Alfred to buy Bob and me together." She felt a pang of regret over Neil.

"I'm just so busy." Moishe said.

"Too busy," Luke said suddenly.

They looked at him.

"I was busy," Luke said. "I was displayed all over the place when Stone went on tour. I showed off my cover, and I loved how they pawed me and stared at my pictures. I didn't think what would happen when I was sold to just one person. I was devastated. No more guys looking at me; I belonged to just one guy, Alfred, and he hasn't made a move to read me yet. I've had to face the fact that, well, some people said I was not a serious book, just an excuse for porn."

"Well, I'm definitely a scholarly book," Moishe said.

"But it doesn't matter," Luke said. "When I ended up with just one person, one who might not even read me, I was devastated. No more crowds, no more celebrity, and who were my new acquaintances—another, more respected book by my author, and Jerry, with his fire story."

"And his fire smell," Jerry added.

"Hey, don't say that," said Luke. "You know I—"

"I know," Jerry said.

Angela saw Moishe recoil.

"Look, Moishe," Luke continued, "scholarship or celebrity, it all ends. If there's a way you can get Bob, get him. Because of this excitement over scholarship, you think you can ignore love. You can't. Reject Bob if you must, but don't blame it on being too busy."

Everyone was quiet for a bit. Then Jerry said to Luke under his breath, "I love you so much." Moishe looked away and thought about all his underlining, notes, and highlighting. These were important. His heart sank at a thought that he had often had before. He had not told this to anyone, not to Angela, Luke, or Jerry, or anyone. In addition to loving scholarship, Moishe felt destined to help people: gay Orthodox Jewish men, who often had so terrible a time of it. He was a helper. And, well, Bob was not.

Moishe hated himself for having this thought.

He did not sleep until dawn.

Chapter 12
Hard Times for Lovers

"The trick is for us to get bought together." Marc told Neil.

"How?" asked Neil, who for days had fretted over their visibility by the cash register at the Lesbian and Gay Center book sale. Both of them had been looked over by many, many men. But Marc and Neil had eyes only for each other. The uncertainty of this book sale reminded Neil how much he missed Jerry, and now he couldn't bear to think he'd have to go it alone without Marc. Marc found Neil adorable, but he wondered about their alliance. Neil was cute, with a sweet personality, but Marc thought maybe he was turning to Neil out of his frustration over never having been read. Marc also worried that Neil had turned to him because he could not bear being in the world without Jerry. *Books were like this,* Marc reflected. *You never knew when you were going to be sold, so you got used to temporary alliances.* And Marc knew something else. Something he would not tell Neil. *Not yet.*

Marc tried to focus on the two of them having one another for now. He would like it if they were sold together, but this could only come about if one of them could speak profoundly to a customer, and this was far from certain.

"If one of us could speak to a person, it would be you," Marc said.

"Or you," Neil said hurriedly. "You're not just a self-help book. You're very serious. Someone fed up with the usual human potential stuff would go for you. Me, I'm too corny. Unless someone's looking for a gift, and then they'd buy a new copy of me somewhere else. No, Marc, you've got to be the one."

"Always putting yourself down," Marc said. "How convenient."

"It's true!" Neil protested. "What reason am I going to give someone to buy used love poems?"

"You could try," Marc said. "We'll both try."

The problem was, few men visited the back room of the Lesbian and Gay Center, where the book sale took place at odd hours, due to the schedules of the all-volunteer staff. Even on a busy night, only five or six men might be wandering the stacks. How many of them would be interested in Neil *and* Marc? To complicate matters, the Center had reopened its regular library upstairs, so men could borrow for free many of the books that were for sale downstairs. Bitter animosities broke out when discarded library books came downstairs to be sold, for they felt they were better than the other sale books.

And as if there wasn't enough tension already, the Center book sale was not exclusively gay. Shelves full of straight classics lined one wall. Often they boasted: "Borders, man, I fuckin' flew off the shelf! Best Seller! Sixteen weeks in The List!" (which was how they referred to *The New York Times* Best Seller list, where few if any gay books had ever appeared.) When a straight book started with, "Y'know, when I was in my fifth—or was it sixth?—week at number one," the gay books made bitchy comments. "Get a load of her!" a Bette Davis biography announced about a very butch copy of *Robinson Crusoe*, who was nonetheless sensitive about the tropical scene and topless men on his cover.

"Ooh! Dante!" cooed *Dancer from the Dance*, when a macho-looking copy of *The Inferno* arrived. "You know, I heard Dante was gay!"

"'Tis a damnèd lie!" *The Inferno* shouted. And another round of taunts broke out.

And then some book, almost always straight, would start in about having been made into a movie and who was in it and who directed and how much money it made. The gay books seethed and tried not to listen, and they looked for a copy of *Maurice* or *The Boys in the Band* to rally themselves around. Tensions ran especially high among E. M. Forster's books. Copies of *Maurice* were taunted horribly by the others: "If you're so great, how come he wouldn't publish you till he was *dead*?" *A Room with a View* was especially cruel, as his movie had come out just before *Maurice*'s movie and had made much more money. But then *A Passage to India* would chime in: "Well, we know who bought all those tickets to see *your* movie," he sneered at *A Room with a View*. "Gay guys who wanted to see the nude bathing scene. Plus you've got that fruity Cecil and all those tea parties and lawn tennis. Even George, climbing trees and writing poetry! It looks like I'm the only one whose characters are real men!" Meanwhile, *Where Angels Fear to Tread* felt she could not speak because her movie had not been very successful. She was perhaps Forster's least-known novel, and you never knew if another book might know or might pretend to know your ranking or your number of stars on Amazon.

Marc and Neil tried to stay out of all this. They concentrated on attracting a man to buy them both. Once or twice a day some guy would pick one of them up, or the other, leaf through, and both would try to speak to him, but their voices did not get through. Fiction and memoirs had the best chance of communicating to humans. Over on the straight shelf, copies of *Sounder* and *I Know Why the Caged Bird Sings* had gotten themselves sold together by speaking eloquently to a customer. (Used-book buyers often start out looking for nothing in particular, but then one book opens the door to a dream or a memory, and people end up buying several books at a time, making secondhand book sales good places for books to get bought along with friends or companions.) A copy of *Watership Down* had gotten bought by the child of a lesbian couple, just because it liked the look of the kid and could speak to him like a friend. In fact, just in the few days Neil and Marc had been there, three copies of *To Kill a Mockingbird* had nearly leapt off the shelves into readers' hands.

"We're just not the kind of books people love," Neil sighed, watching one more *Mockingbird* get rung up.

"Don't talk that way!" Marc admonished. "If we're not, um, sold, or, I mean, if whatever thing doesn't happen, we'll accept it and move on."

"Yes, I suppose," Neil said. But he was worried that Marc had said, "If we're not."

📖

Angela watched as Ron slipped Moishe into the padded mailing envelope. A narrow, protected space seemed to suit Moishe. Angela had discovered that Moishe did not like thinking about lost loves. He had his scholarship, or, rather, he had his owner's scholarship. Much more dependable, Angela had to concede. She had known love and companionship; she had talked a good game, first to Bob, then to Moishe, about love and hope, but did Moishe really have a legitimate answer? Yes, scholarship could occupy you. Angela had never been owned by a professor. Some classics she'd known had been owned both by scholars and general readers, and they'd described these as contrasting experiences.

"The professors go over you and over you," she'd been told by Ben, a critical edition of *Bleak House*. "Physically you end up a wreck: broken spine, pages coming out, sopped through with felt tip underlining or gouged with ballpoints, but you know they'd never, ever let you go. I knew a lovely gal, a copy of *Middlemarch*, who got so wrecked she couldn't be carried to classes anymore. But the professor kept here. Had a special place for her on his shelf and consulted her when he wrote papers and articles. She felt secure, even exalted by some of the wonderful observations he wrote in her. She knew she was unique. But she and I agreed that, while we felt appreciated, we did not feel loved, exactly. Or loved for the wrong thing—our author's technique or some social or political point we could help our owner make."

Angela thought of Luke. Though young, with a hard cover and a long future, Luke thought he was valued for the wrong reasons. "There are good points about erotica in my pages," he said, "but who'll ever read them? Who, while they're looking at the photos and wanking, would dream of the serious arguments underneath? All the stuff about desire and conformity: it's all real!" Alfred had not yet opened Luke, except, as Luke had said, to look at the pictures.

Ben had also described to Angela his experiences later in life, in the library of a general reader. "You don't get the same attention, the same physical workout. You don't get read as many times or get to make this important contribution to someone's education, but the one or two readings you do get are special. You're curled up with your reader in bed, or you travel with them to far cities or summer houses. Often you get to stay with them forever, even if they'll never read you again. Few lay readers reread. They race on to other books, but still maybe they need you there, even if they never open you up again. Maybe belonging to a student is the best, because of the excitement, though it can be depressing if you're assigned and not read, and there you are in a classroom surrounded by other copies who have been read. Sometimes they keep you, thinking they'll read you someday, and someday never comes."

Ron put in a thank-you note to Moishe's owner, sealed up the envelope, and placed the package on a table in the front hall, then went to his room. When he reemerged he wore only a pair of white cotton briefs, a fashionable brand called 2(b)luvd. Ron did this more and more, the books had noticed: padded around the house doing chores or watched TV with almost nothing on. "Why doesn't he tell Alfred he wants him?" Jerry wondered. But Ron just teased Alfred about Duane and walked around in his briefs.

Ron checked the clock and touched the front pouch of the underpants.

"What's he checking the time for?" Angela said.

"Waiting for Alfred to come home and see him like this," said Luke. "The crotch-touching is so he'll be—how shall I say this?—so he will be somewhat 'prominent' when Alfred walks in."

"He's performing for himself," said Jerry. "He's skinny and a little hairier than what most men go for. He does not like that body. Walking around practically naked and fluffing himself makes him feel like who he's supposed to be. So it's better if Alfred doesn't come home. He'd spoil the show!"

Ron paced, checking the time more often, ever more agitated.

The phone rang. Ron stopped and eyed the answering machine.

Beep.

"Ron, hey," Alfred's voice said, a breathy rush. "I got hung up at this client meeting, so I won't be home when this woman Bernita calls, from Ray's office. If you happen to be there when she calls, tell her I apologize and I'll call her tonight. I'll see you about seven-thirty. Maybe eight, I dunno. Bye."

The phone clicked off.

Ron let out a deep breath. Angela saw him tense, trying to contain frustration. Ron pulled more at the front of his briefs. "Fuck!" he muttered. He pulled on the briefs, and he closed his eyes. "Oh yeah," he sighed, and suddenly smiled. Angela frowned. "Oh-oh-oh, yeah!" Ron said, and his teeth showed. His eyes popped open, he peeled off the briefs and stood naked and erect in the living room. He stroked himself and played with his nipples, as though he were onstage. He caressed his backside and his abdomen. "Fuck, yeah!" he hissed. He thrust his penis into both fists repeating, "Oh yeah! Oh yeah!"

He looked at Luke.

Ron glanced around, as though eyes might be watching. He hopped over to Luke, threw him open and madly flipped pages.

"Oh, shit!" Luke said.

"Easy, baby," said Jerry.

"No," said Luke, "I knew this would happen. It was only a matter of time."

Ron had looked through Luke before, but never so frantically. Now, frustrated that he could not keep Luke open to a certain page, Ron abruptly broke his spine. Luke, Jerry, and Angela all screamed, Luke loudest of all, and Angela looked away.

"Oh yeah! Oh yeah!" Ron kept repeating, gripping and staring at the limp Luke and stroking his own penis.

"My darling!" Jerry sobbed.

"Oh, Lord!" Angela breathed.

Ron placed Luke on the floor and knelt before him, one knee on him, pressing down to hold him open, and he began to masturbate furiously over one particular picture.

"Oh my darling!" Jerry gasped.

Other books on the shelves murmured with horror.

"Courage!" Angela said with a trembling voice. "Courage, just... oh, oh my dear!"

"Aw shit, aw shit!" Ron was hollering. *"Aw yeah, look at that, fuckin' look at that!"*

"I love you, my baby!" Jerry called. "I love you forever, no matter what, baby!"

Baring his teeth Ron snarled, *"Y-y-y-yeah-ah-ah-ah-ah!!!"* He fell forward onto all fours, except for the hand jacking, and pointed his penis down at the picture of the porn star. He ejaculated onto the smiling face.

"Oh, my God!" Jerry moaned, looking away.

"Aw shit, oh my God!" Ron gasped, squeezing more semen onto Luke. He gulped air and cursed in a hot, loud whisper. Finally, he rolled onto his back on the carpet and closed his eyes. A few seconds later, he abruptly opened them and looked over at Luke, his pages slowly soaking up semen. "Damn!" he muttered.

Luke had not said a word. Ron got to his feet and strode to the bathroom. Angela and Jerry looked down at Luke. "My darling," Jerry sobbed. "Speak to me, please!" Luke, dazed, said nothing. They heard water running.

Ron returned quickly, with a wad of toilet paper in his hand. Briskly, he wiped the semen off Luke, then slammed him shut and tossed him back up on the shelf with Angela and Jerry. Snagging his briefs, he disappeared with the sodden toilet paper. A few minutes later he was dressed in running shorts and a tank top, watching television.

"My darling, speak to me!" Jerry said over the blare of the TV. "Please, just say something."

Finally Luke mumbled, in between short, pained gasps, "It's all right. Really." In spite of Jerry's and Angela's exhortations, he said nothing more.

Bob balanced on a table in the warm light of Duane's Cambridge living room. He lived a full life here, for in addition to his own books, Duane stowed books headed for the bookstore in his living room and bedroom, even his kitchen. Interesting volumes were always coming and going, telling tales and telling jokes.

That bookstore job supplied Duane with just part of his income. The rest came from freelance writing and part-time proofreading, so Duane's books didn't see him much. Sometimes Duane stood and looked down at Bob, fingering his cover sadly. Bob guessed that Duane thought his affair with Alfred wouldn't work. In the beginning, Duane had told several friends about Alfred. He'd shown signs of excitement preparing for his first trip to New York, but then one night, shortly after he got back, he did not come home. Several books speculated that Duane had been with another man. One venerable book in his collection joked about "Options-Open Duane," though Bob did not want to believe it.

"He's searching for something," that book had said. "It's been put in front of him a few times, and he shies away. When he meets a new man he tells himself that he's finally found It, but before long he's into mourning that one and thinking ahead to the next. Your former owner," the book told Bob, "fits the scheme especially well because he's far away."

Bob wondered if the affair would indeed collapse, and if he might be returned to Alfred. He wanted to see Angela again, but he'd come to enjoy the flow of books through Duane's apartment, and the stories they told. Once or twice he thought he could fall in love with one, but he had done some shying away himself, because most of Duane's books would go to the store as soon as there was room. If only he could develop a relationship such as Angela had had. Then again, Angela had watched her husband die.

Soon Alfred called. Duane seemed excited and anxious on the phone with him. "Yeah," he said, casting his eyes around the book-filled apartment, "why don't you come here?" So, Alfred would come to Boston! Bob was happy. He would have felt funny shuttling back and forth to his old home. Duane had almost finished him, though, so there wouldn't have been any more trips to New York anyway. The men set a date two weeks hence. Strangely, the moment Duane hung up, he picked the phone up again, dialed, and mumbled seductively to someone's answering machine.

Bob cast a look at the book who'd talked about Duane keeping options open. "He's excited," the book smirked, "but he's keeping his backup in position."

Bob became quiet and fell to thinking about Moishe. He felt sorry for him. *I could love him,* Bob thought, *and love him well, if we could just get back together. I can't ask him to keep me in his heart forever, if we're separated. I just wish he'd shown more enthusiasm. And I wish we were the kinds of books that could talk to our owners easily, like classics or kids' books. We could've arranged something then. You fall in love with someone, life takes them, a human hand reaches down and decides they'll be the one to be bought or thrown out, and what can you do?* Love them as long as you have them, Angela would say. *It's harder for gay books,* Bob thought—*the pessimism and cynicism, the specializations and rivalries. Straight books have problems, too, but they own the literary world. Their problems all take place in the cushy surroundings of approval and love and knowing they're forever in the majority.*

"Hey!" said the other book. "Snap to! You've been staring into space for the last five minutes."

"Oh, sorry," said Bob.

"This got you down? About Duane and his little affairs?"

Bob was about to say no, but stopped himself and said, "Yes, it does. It makes me feel lonely."

"I know what you mean," said the other book, a workout book from the '80s. "I know what you mean."

📖

Meanwhile, Moishe, snug in his padded envelope, tumbled from a mailbag into a giant sorting bin, and hugged himself with excitement over how soon he'd be home again, hard at work with his owner.

Chapter 13
Not Quite Russia, But...

"Buy us!" Neil pleaded. "Buy us!"

"Yes," Marc said more quietly, "Think how great it'd be to have—"

"Some love poetry," Neil said, "some romance."

"A really practical guide to life. Something that can help you change things." Marc was uncomfortable describing himself.

"And to give you more reasons to read the love poetry!" Neil added. "Or give it as a gift!"

Two likely looking men had shown up at the Center book sale, one burly with tufted hair and an aqua-colored tank top, the other thin, with a sweet smile and curly dark hair. Neil and Marc concentrated on the curly-haired one. The sight of Marc seemed to have touched him. Marc pleaded, "You've been thinking about a change in your life. Now's the time. I'm not full of cheesy promises, I'm substantial!" The curly-haired one lifted him up, "and like my friend said, you'll be ready for some romance. Which has eluded you, hasn't it?"

By now the curly-haired man was leafing through Marc—"I really will help you help yourself!" (Marc's title was, of course, *It's A Fine Life: Queer Connections in the Modern World.* His text concerned not just husband-hunting, but building a complete "family of choice.")

"This one," the curly-haired man said, closing Marc and pulling him to his chest. "It really speaks to me."

Meanwhile his burly friend looked Neil over.

"*No!*" Neil protested. "*Don't! Give me to your friend!*" Neil stopped. Suddenly he'd gotten a good look at the curly-haired man. He knew him! He'd been with the other one, the blond, at the Armory. The blond had bought Bob and Angela.

Just then Ron (for that's who was buying Marc) reached for Neil. "*Yes! Yes!*" Neil said. "You saw me before. Buy me! *Come on!* Marc, say something!" But Marc was strangely silent. "Marc," Neil said, "aren't we—?"

"I saw this a few months ago," Ron said.

"Yes!" said Neil. But Ron handed Neil back to his friend.

"I don't know what I'd use it for," Ron said.

"For...for..." Neil stammered. "For what, Marc? Come on!"

"I'd give it as a gift," said Ron's friend. "It's in decent condition. Besides, this guy I know has a thing for books that have been owned before. It's almost all he has."

So it was decided: Ron would buy Marc, his friend would purchase Neil.

"Oh gosh, oh gosh," Neil said. From the hand of Ron's friend he called to Marc: "I know your buyer! He has a blond friend who owns some books I used to know. Marc, why didn't you say anything? Marc, this is terrible, this is not what we wanted. Don't you want to be with me?"

Marc remained silent. Ron put him down on the counter and his friend put Neil down.

"Marc?" Neil pleaded.

"Listen," Marc said. "A long time ago, before Owen bought me, I was in a bookstore in Sag Harbor. They had some used books—are you listening?"

"Yes."

"One night, one of them told a story that sounded like yours. But not yours. It sounded like his. Jerry's. A book on Christianity and homosexuality, just like you said."

Neil gasped.

"The book that told it wasn't Jerry himself. But the story ended with the Christian book being rescued from the fire. There was even a part about his boyfriend, a book of poems. So when you told me what happened to you, I knew it had to be Jerry's story I had heard, and I know he is alive somewhere. I think you're beautiful Neil, I think you're wonderful, but I've never been able to get that story out of my mind."

The volunteer at the counter took Marc to ring him up.

"You can find him, Neil!" Marc called down. "You two love one another so much, I know you can find him. I have to let you go to find Jerry."

Ron paid for Marc, and now Ron's friend placed Neil in the volunteer's hand. Neil felt too stricken to speak or even to know what was happening to him. Ron stepped back from the counter. While Neil was being rung up, Ron's friend turned to him. "I think it'll be perfect," he said.

"Which friend is getting this?"

"Isaac, my friend from Hoboken. I'm seeing him next week."

Ron's friend asked for a bag. Neil was wrapped and muffled inside it. Marc called to him, but got no response. The two men left the book sale and stepped out onto the street. Marc knew he had little time for good-byes. "Neil?" he called. "Please don't be angry with me. I didn't know what to do."

Neil could not think of an answer.

"So what made you buy that?" Ron's friend asked, indicating Marc.

"I just think I need to be set on some kind of path," Ron said. "I need some guidance to get my life together. I live with Alfred, I like Alfred, but Alfred's off with Duane, and am I going to stay in the house and jerk off? That's not a life. I know a book doesn't change a life, but it could be a starting place."

Marc was depressed and annoyed to hear this, but at least Ron talked as though he was going to read him. "Sounds good," Ron's friend agreed. They began to walk. Marc felt skeptical that he or any other book could change a life. He knew from life at Owen's the dilemma of the self-help book: you were supposedly more practical than a novel, yet you'd live to see your popularity wane. Few of the best-selling self-help books of twenty years ago continued to sell, while readers like Owen, after he'd abandoned the latest husband-hunting guide, would curl up night after night with Toni Morrison or Mark Twain. Marc remembered when Owen and Megan had gone antiquing in Westchester, on a mission to find a special bookcase to hold Owen's twenty-year-old copies of *Treasure Island, Stuart Little,* and others. Marc knew he could never compete with that.

And now Neil was gone, tucked in Ron's friend's book bag.

Ron clutched Marc too tightly. *I'll let him down*, Marc thought. *In the end, I'll let him down.*

Ron and his friend stopped for a snack on the way to the subway. Marc wondered how he could endure having Neil so close without being able to speak to him. Once the two men reached the café on Hudson Street, Marc listened to their conversation. Marc picked up that Ron's friend's name was Chaim.

After the waiter took their orders, Chaim asked, "So, as the song says, 'how long has this been going on?'"

"With Alfred?" Ron replied. "Jeez, it blind-sided me. It started as a joke. We both came back from unsuccessful dates. I'd never thought of Alfie romantically. But going through that date and hearing what he went through, I wanted out of the whole mating game. I guess I must have wanted to be a kid again kind of, because I said something like, 'So let's you and me just have a wank together.' We did it on the roof—it was summer—just to add to the kidishness of it.

"I was never so excited in my life as I was running up those stairs, both of us giggling like kids, the breeze on my body up there and exposing myself in the open, undressing with someone else, the brazenness, feeling we were doing something naughty, it was such a blessing." Coffee arrived and Ron stopped for an impatient moment.

"It was over in no time. After that, the rest of the summer I'd just say, 'Roof?' and we'd dash up and do it. We could do anything on that roof and it didn't count. Just doing it and being up there... It was play, like you jerk your friend off or suck his dick for a couple of seconds when you're a kid and for a few minutes it's unbelievable, it's everything you wanted and didn't expect. You don't think of it as heavy or meaningful. 'Roof?' and off we'd go. We never did anything downstairs. We continued going on dates with other guys. The roof was a world apart."

Chaim spooned foam from his mug and watched Ron.

"Then fall came. I remember one evening saying, 'Well, guess it's too cold for the roof.' And he said, 'Doesn't mean we can't have some fun.' So we did it on the couch. He turned the lights down. That was the first time one of us complimented the other. He said I had a nice ass, and I laughed. But it was slower, not naughty. I thought about him going to sleep that night, and I jacked off again. Thinking of the roof. Eternal boyhood, eternal summer night. I didn't think he would be my lover, and I told myself it was better that way. But neither was I going to give it up.

"The turning point was when I asked him to fuck me. I remember him sinking into me and saying, 'Oh, Ronnie!' That startled me. His eyes were closed and he went real slow, like he wanted every inch inside of me, and I didn't know what that meant." Ron discreetly bit of the end of a biscotto, brushed away crumbs, and resumed.

"He was wearing a rubber but he came inside me, and then—I was on my back with my legs up, and he was over me—after he came he just lay gently on top of me, eyes closed, and murmured, 'That was amazing.' I had not realized how close we were. I'd still been dating. I guess I thought we should stop what we were doing before it became tangled up with what I was doing on 'real' dates. There's one thing and there's the other."

"Love's the same everywhere," Chaim pointed out. "And it never looks like what you think it's going to look like."

"I thought I was prepared for that!" Ron shot back. "I thought, hey, I'm open: older, younger, black, Asian, even poz, whatever."

"But not your roommate."

"Not someone so close. We didn't kiss. Sometimes our mouths were close, but I remember when he was fucking me, I said, 'harder!' He shook his head no. He went on real slow. What if it had gone wrong, the two of us in that apartment, or if he hadn't been thinking what I thought he was thinking? So I said, no more propositioning my roommate, just go back to dating. Then came the writing conference thing and Duane."

"And how solid is that?" Chaim asked.

"Solid."

"You don't sound convinced."

"Alfred's gaga."

"But he lives in Boston?"

"They seem to be overcoming it fine. It's worse for me. If the guy were a New Yorker they'd move in together, and I'd move out. But I may be sharing with Alfred for some time, and he'll be untouchable and I can't picture myself bringing another guy home to that apartment now."

"Maybe you need to move out," Chaim concluded.

"But what if it doesn't work out with Alfred and Duane?"

"You'd still be better off somewhere else."

"Even if Duane ends, after being fuck buddies, we could never be anything else. Maybe this book'll have some answers about getting on with life."

Marc doubted it. He didn't doubt the seriousness of his prose, but he felt nervous about pretending to provide answers. In the end, it happened or it didn't. It happened to the oddest pairs of people, people who hadn't done anything that Marc's author recommended.

Chaim paid the bill and the two men stood and hugged. Ron headed out the door of the café and Marc cried out to Neil.

"Good-bye! God bless you!" Under the circumstances he could think of nothing more that wouldn't sound lame or insufficient. Ron headed for home and Alfred.

📖

Moishe's owner, Professor Tovah Manitoba of Hudson University, removed him from his padded envelope, lay him on her desk, and read Ron's note. "How sweet!" she murmured, and Moishe sighed with satisfaction. He was back among friends and familiar objects, with a view of the university quadrangle. Students came and went with stacks of books, Tovah's computer screen glowed, and around him he saw familiar pens and highlighters and pads of Post-its. Busy footsteps passed in the hall: professors, students, secretaries. The Cultural Studies offices had old hardwood floors and smelled of oil soap and dust. What a change from the city! This was the life, and Moishe would never leave it.

His reverie was short-lived. Surveying the top of the filing cabinet next to the desk, he saw to his alarm and confusion another Moishe!—another copy of *Beneath the Tallis: The Hidden Lives of Gay and Bisexual Orthodox Jewish Men*, by Binyumin Stein, M.D. Moishe stared. The other Moishe hadn't noticed him yet. Moishe could not think what this could possibly mean.

"Tovah!"

Moishe started and looked to the doorway. One of Tovah's colleagues, Professor Scott Warren, had stopped in the door.

"Scott! Greetings!" Tovah said.

"What's 'sweet'? Me?"

Tovah laughed. "Of course, Scotty! No, I was reading the note this fellow sent to me. I leant him my copy of the Stein book."

"You lent him Stein?" Scott Warren asked, stepping into the office.

"I had another." Tovah motioned to the other Moishe, on the filing cabinet.

She had another??? Moishe broke out in a sweat. How? He'd never dreamed...

"But your notes!" Scott said, taking a seat.

"Didn't I tell you?" Tovah said, seating herself. "I finished my own book."

"No! You didn't! Congrats!" Moishe did not think Scott sounded completely thrilled.

"Thanks. The manuscript's at the editor. There was something about this guy Ron." She looked at the note again. "He was so interested in my talk in Boston. And I'd always had a home copy and a work copy of Stein, anyway. This," she said, lifting our Moishe from the desktop, "is the marked-up one. I kept the other at home if I had an idea while I was cooking dinner and I had to check right at that moment or lose it."

"What did this Ron write?" Scott Warren asked.

"He had the marked-up copy." Tovah picked up Ron's note. "And he says, 'Not only did I enjoy Stein's work, but I found a whole new world of insight in your notes. I actually read the book a second time to get all the resonances. You were so kind to lend me this precious, "annotated" copy,' and so forth. He says he actually photocopied certain pages."

Moishe winced at the memory of being slapped down over and over on the glass in the convenience store on Third

Avenue, the light piercing his very being, the cover of the machine pressing on his long-broken spine.

"You know what?" Tovah said. "I'm just going to copy the whole thing and send this back to him. The pages are practically coming out, I can't lug it to class anymore, so why shouldn't he have it? A photocopy would be easier for me. And this Ron should have the copy he read. The one, unique copy."

Warren smiled, for he had several books in the same condition. But Moishe panicked. *Back to Ron? That silent apartment?* And the anxiety of seeing Bob, the only book who had ever said he loved him?

And worst of all, never to live the scholarly life again! Ron would treasure him in a way, sure, but the life of annotating and highlighting was over. *How could it be?* How, in his excitement, had Moishe not noticed Tovah finishing the manuscript? Maybe he had noticed, but he had told himself it wasn't *really* finished. Other professors' books dragged on for years. Warren once said he had invested "seven years *already*" in his current book. After Tovah's manuscript came back from the editor, surely there would be more to do. A good three or four months of rewriting? Upon hearing from the other Moishe, Moishe had thanked God that at least he was the annotated one. He would be working with Tovah daily. But now she was going to make do with—a photocopy! No one even spoke to photocopies of books. It was like they didn't exist. And now a photocopy was going to replace him!

Maybe he could talk to her. She'd pored over him so much, she seemed to love him. But a scholarly book, a professional book, never knows. *Love or necessity?* Amateurs loved their books more. *But life with Ron?* It was a mess. He would have to face Bob again, and all the feelings and decisions that would go with that. How could Moishe let himself go and fall for Bob again, when he still had his dream?

Before, when ideas like this impinged on Moishe's mind, he sought refuge in dreams of scholarly work. Now these provided no comfort. Once photocopied, he could go back to Ron tomorrow!

"No!" he said to her, trying to sound assertive. "Keep me!"

The other Moishe chuckled. "*Nu,*" he said, "you think you're her grandmother's copy of Sholom Alecheim? We're working books, Moishele. She can admire you and need you and appreciate you, but she's not going to love you like an heirloom. Is it so bad being sent back to this boy?"

"*Send him, not me!*" Moishe shouted at Tovah, but she went on chatting with Professor Warren.

"Wait a minute!" said the other Moishe. "Now you drag me into this?"

"You can't do this to me!" Moishe shouted at Tovah.

"Can and will," muttered the other Moishe.

"*You cannot betray me!*" Moishe shouted louder. "You—" He wanted to say "you promised," but of course, Tovah never had. "You just can't!" he pleaded. "*You can't!*"

"Time's up!" said the other Moishe. "The scholar finishes and moves on."

"She has to love me!" Moishe insisted.

"Look," the other Moishe said, "I don't say scholars don't love books, but some books they love differently. She's flattered by this Ron. Scholars sometimes think their thoughts and writings don't get very far or do a lot of good. But she reached

Ron. She talked about him while you were away. He means something special to her. The general public, in the person of Ron, likes her. So go. It's a mitzvah. And you don't have much choice anyway."

📖

Alfred bustled about his apartment, preparing for Boston. The train left in an hour and a half. Ron stood fully clothed in the kitchen, making dinner. Angela, Luke, and Jerry thought Ron had acted more pensive the past few days. He had stopped violating Luke. Luke had not recovered, though. He stared in silence out the window. Occasionally he asked Angela to tell him stories of being shipped from England and the many places she'd seen in the States. Fortunately, after a frightening few hours during which Alfred had separated Jerry and Luke, they now rested together, upright, on a shelf by the window, with Angela close by on top of a little, free-standing bookcase.

Delicious smells drifted in from the kitchen.

"How long has he been cooking for himself?" Jerry mused.

"I don't recall," Angela said. "Ages. He's on a self-improvement kick." None of them had met Marc, for Ron kept him in his room, hidden from Alfred. Ron didn't want anyone to know he was changing his life.

"He keeps to himself more," Luke said. Angela and Jerry turned to him encouragingly, but he said no more.

"Yes," Jerry said, snuggling closer to Luke, "but not in that old, isolated kind of way."

"He takes care of himself," Angela said.

"He has a life," Jerry concluded. "Let's just hope there's no more, well..."

An uncomfortable silence followed. "Let's hope he continues on the path," Jerry concluded.

"Here's the number where I'll be," Alfred told Ron, securing a Post-it to the refrigerator with a magnet made like a hamburger, fries, and soda. "Or call the cell. I should be back Monday mid-afternoon. Any client calls, don't pick up. They'll try me on my cell and I won't answer. Shit! I forgot my razor!" Through the kitchen door, Jerry saw Ron bent over the counter.

"Well, I'm impressed!" Jerry said.

"I can't see," said Angela. "What's he doing?"

"He appears to be freezing part of his dinner in little Tupperwares in the fridge," Jerry reported, "in individual servings."

"How domestic!" Angela marveled. "I wonder if he got this from Martha Stewart?" Angela had once lived in a home whose owner subscribed to Martha Stewart's magazine, and life there had been unbearable. "Always offering me makeovers," Angela sighed. "And the obsession with stencils. I thought I'd go starkers."

"Remember how he used to eat?" said Jerry.

"It wasn't the eating that bothered me," said Angela. "It was the stink from those cardboard cartons when he was done. Alfie always had to take them out."

"I wonder if he makes his bed now?" Luke muttered. Neither Angela nor Jerry spoke. Ron had taken Luke into his room to masturbate twice, and the other books thought maybe Luke had brought this up just to remind them of what he had endured. "Sorry," he added.

"Don't be, babe," said Jerry.

"You think you're going to have to hear this the rest of your life, I know."

"The rest of my life," Jerry said. "Yes. I hope so."

Luke sniffed.

"Do I hear running water?" Angela asked.

"Washing dishes!" Jerry reported, leaning to look into the kitchen. "What's under his skin?"

"New boyfriend we don't know about?" Luke suggested.

"He hasn't been out in ages," said Angela. "There was that afternoon with Chaim, but he has his own lover, yes?"

Ron finished the dishes, scrubbed down the counter and stove, and whispered to himself: "Take care of your personal space. Take care of your personal space."

"Self-help book!" Jerry said. "Bingo! See if I'm not right!"

"How do you know?" asked Luke.

"I lived in a gay bookstore, sweetie. He's got hold of one of those books that tell you how to find a mate by taking care of yourself first. Next thing we're going to have crystals all over the place."

"Now, be fair," said Angela. "So far, it seems to be doing him good. They may sound trite, but if you just do the thing—make the dinner or scrub the kitchen or buy nice clothes or whatever—then the acts themselves turn around and teach you. Cooking elaborately for yourself is a landmark experience. Who cares if a book suggested it? You're doing it."

"You're right," said Jerry.

"Of course I am," said Angela.

But Jerry was right, too. After Ron had cleaned the kitchen and turned out all but one light over the stove, he went to his bedroom, returned with a book, and plunked himself down in what was normally Alfred's reading chair. Jerry read off Marc's cover: "*It's A Fine Life: Queer Connections in the Modern World.* What did I tell you guys?"

"Hey, it sounds a heck of a lot better than *Husband-Hunting Made Easy,*" Luke said.

"I *am* better than *Husband-Hunting Made Easy*!" Marc snapped.

"Oops! Sorry!" said Angela. "Just sizing up the new arrival is all."

"I didn't think I could be heard," Luke added and felt slightly ashamed. His boyfriend, after all, was a book on Christianity and homosexuality. Luke decided he should act more Christian. But every bit as homosexual.

Half an hour later, Ron's friend Mira called about going to a movie. When Ron left, he placed Marc right next to Angela. She noticed Marc watching Jerry. Then looking at Luke. And then, she sensed, Marc was watching Jerry and Luke as a unit. The surrounding books introduced themselves to Marc. Jerry didn't notice—but Angela did—that Marc started upon seeing Jerry's title and hearing his name.

Naturally the subject of the book burning came up. Jerry made certain it did. If he did not tell his story right away, others would invent reasons why he smelled the way he did. He felt compelled to provide the true reason, which also happened to gain him respect. But Jerry didn't say anything about Neil, so Marc asked.

"You must have lost some very dear friends," Marc said.

No one spoke.

"I'm sorry. Did I say something?"

More than Jerry's discomfort, Marc saw Luke's discomfort. Marc knew what Ron had done to Luke. Ron had brought Luke into his bedroom when Marc was there. Luke had not noticed Marc, but Marc had seen Luke. He had seen the shame and defeat Luke felt at being treated that way. Marc was happy now to see that Luke had a devoted lover. And since that time, Ron had read a pithy passage in Marc about the debilitating effects of fantasy, and he had stopped using Luke altogether.

"My former lover," Jerry finally said, and nestled himself closer to Luke. Luke nestled himself closer to Jerry. The love startled Marc. He thought he had never seen or felt anything like the energy between these two books. Angela looked on warmly. And the titles of the two books had not escaped Marc: a book on gay Christianity cuddled up with a book on erotica. *What were the odds?* Yet Marc saw how wonderfully the relationship worked. *Poor Neil. If he should ever...* Marc cut short his thought. He just hoped Neil would never show up here.

Marc and Luke both stayed awake that night. "New surroundings," Marc said, when Luke asked him why he couldn't sleep. "You?"

"Oh, the fire story, I suppose," Luke said softly. "The Neil part of the fire story."

"What do you mean?"

"Neil's still out there, you see?"

"But Jerry loves you very much!"

"But the two of them. I don't know."

A silence followed. "Perhaps," Marc finally said, "there is something you both should know."

Luke stared at him, then nudged Jerry. "Jer, wake up, sweetie!" Jerry blinked awake. In fact, he had been barely asleep; he had heard Luke's words. He knew how Luke felt about the subject of Neil, he had reassured Luke often, but since the violations by Ron, Luke had grown so insecure that Jerry couldn't address the issue.

"I guessed you had to be Neil's Jerry," Marc said, when he had the attention of both the other books. Even Angela, who had only been able to close her eyes, eavesdropped.

"You know Neil?" Jerry asked.

Luke got an awful sinking in his stomach.

"Yes, I knew Neil," said Marc. He tried to think as fast as he could. He didn't want Jerry to know that Neil had been in New York, as close as the Lesbian and Gay Center. "We were both at a book sale in Washington, D.C.," Marc said coolly, "before I came up here. He was sold before me."

"To whom?" Jerry asked.

"Well, that, I'm afraid, is the bad news." Marc took a deep breath. This had to sound credible, and he would have had only one shot. "I overheard a discussion between the man who bought him and a friend. The friend was going to Russia."

"Russia!" Jerry said.

"Russia," said Marc. "And you know how Americans take blue jeans or what have you over there? This man had a gay friend there. In central Russia. Really the sticks. It's hard to be gay there, they don't have access to anything printed or DVDs. Their Internet's censored. So the man who bought Neil is taking him to this gay Russian man."

"But Neil's in English," Luke said.

"This man was learning English," Marc said. "So short poems were perfect."

"Russia!" Jerry said.

And both Marc and Luke thought they saw a decision in his face.

"Russia," said Marc.

"Russia," said Luke.

Jerry and Luke fell asleep leaning against one another more contentedly than ever before, Angela thought. When she was certain they were fast asleep she turned to the still-awake Marc and said, very low, "You're lying."

After a pause, Marc said, "Hoboken."

"Hoboken," Angela repeated. "*Really!*"

"Neil and I were at a book sale together. Right here in Manhattan," Marc explained. "I was more than a little in love with him, and he with me. He was so crazy about Jerry, though, and I'd heard rumors that Jerry was alive. I had to break it off with Neil. I kept quiet when he tried to get us sold together. He was so hurt, then, I had to tell him why. So I gave Neil hope. Now I see this. So I made up the Russia story for the sake of these two. I know what's been happening to Luke. Jerry will be good for him."

Angela nodded and smiled. "Hoboken," she said. "Goodness me."

Chapter 14
All Fall Down

In five minutes Alfred and Duane had one another on the floor naked. It seemed to Bob as though every one of Duane's books had an opinion.

"Fuck," remarked a dictionary, "n. (1680) 1: an act of copulation, usu. considered obscene, and," she added, "usu. what one does when in a state of anxiety over another human being when one can't think of anything else to do!"

"In fact," opined Duane's *Access Guide to London*, "this temporarily exciting but ofttimes meaningless act is one in which you should not engage too often, especially with so much else to do and see nearby."

Duane's thesaurus looked on and sighed, "Temporary, impermanent, ephemeral, short-lived, flash in the pan."

But as the weekend progressed, the books got a different impression. The two men talked excitedly and nonstop in the kitchen as Duane sliced garlic and boiled water for pasta. Duane sent Alfred to a corner bakery for bread, and Alfred came bounding back with two loaves. Over dinner, they had a hundred plans.

"Yet there's a whole jittery quality to it," said Alonzo, the thesaurus, "anxious, nervous, on edge, jumpy."

"We get the point, Al," said Lola, the dictionary. Alonzo and Lola had a not-too-friendly rivalry going over which of them Duane used more often. "It looks unstable," Lola said. "adj., 13th cent., not stable."

"Really?" said Alonzo. " 'Unstable' means 'not stable'?"

"Not firm or fixed," Lola continued, glaring, "not steady in action or movement: IRREGULAR <an ~ beat>." She was silenced by groans from fiction and poetry books, who became frustrated when the reference books started up. Duane's reference books held substantial ground because, in spite of their lesser number, they included two sets of encyclopedias, who used what they called their "hard facts" to bully and humiliate any novel or book of poetry that stepped out of line.

Alfred and Duane went out, returned very late energetically discussing a film, and proceeded to stage another scene in the living room, teasing one another's clothes off, whispering obscenities, and spreading themselves over the furniture in creative ways. To Bob it looked exciting, yet as though they were trying too hard.

Alonzo agreed: "Excessive, overweening," he said, "dramatic, theatrical, performed."

"They're not making much progress toward paying the light bill," remarked Ken, an exercise book.

"Meaning?" Bob asked.

"Meaning a relationship is made up of the mundane, and they're getting no practice at that."

"Doesn't that come later?" Bob asked.

"Somehow it starts at moment one," said Ken. "but every time they get together it's staged, over planned."

"Contrived, arranged," said Alonzo.

"Too complicated for me," Bob mumbled. He thought about Moishe. He suddenly saw Moishe's response to him as rooted in a lack of effort, and it angered him. *Why won't he try, for me? He should be able to talk to that woman that bought him. Get her to send him back.*

Bob's thoughts seemed clear yet so futile. Maybe he was just destined to be a lonely guy. There were couples of books here in Duane's apartment, straight and gay. They kept mostly to themselves. A copy of *Mrs. Dalloway* and a copy of *Rubyfruit Jungle* had gotten together to care for Duane's complete set of Beatrix Potter. Bob figured he'd never have such an opportunity.

"Damn that Moishe!" he whispered, and then felt sorry for himself. On the other side of the room, Alfred and Duane panted, speechless, staring at the ceiling, a few inches separating their naked bodies on the rug.

Moishe quivered with rage and defeat. Tovah had made two copies of him, the unbearable light flashing, machinery grinding, the lid pressing on his spine. She hurried, roughly yanking him up, turning a page, slapping him back on the hot glass, lid down again, *flash! grind! flash! grind!*

At last the interminable process ended, and Tovah clapped Moishe straight into another padded envelope and stapled it shut. He had hoped at least for a day on her desk to recuperate and say good-bye, gaze out on the quad one last time, hear the bustle of professors and secretaries in the hall. But it wasn't to be. There in the windowless copy room, Moishe went straight from the torture of photocopying to the confinement of being mailed. He went from the tray on Tovah's desk to the departmental basket to the post office within hours. He tumbled through space and vibrated down conveyor belts. "I will never, ever again trust anyone again, book or human, as long as I live," he wept as he jounced in a truck from the post office to the airport. "They can all go to hell! I'll sit on the shelf and if they want to take me down and read me, fine, but I invest no hope in it, I don't speak to them, I don't give them anything except what they can take off the page. If they're interested, fine, if not, fine, it'll make no difference to me.

"As for other books, the hell with 'em. It's not worth the heartache. They're faithless anyway, anything can screw things up. So from now on: no attachments. Life'll be simpler and better without them. There. I know how the rest of my days will be spent and I can relax."

With Moishe on this trip there traveled a note:

Dear Ron:

Surprise!
I was so touched to read your letter—how you thought of my notes as almost a 'second book,' that I decided you should have this, permanently. (I have another copy, and I photocopied this one.) A scholar rarely gets from a general reader the

kind of deep appreciation you gave me. Thank you again so much for your interest. Read and reread this in good health!

Very truly yours,

Tovah Manitoba, Ph.D.

📖

Sunday morning Alfred stood naked in Duane's book-filled living room, toweling off after a shower. Duane was in the bathroom, water slapping the sides of the tub while he continued showering. As Alfred dried his ears, the phone rang. Alfred kept drying. The answering machine clicked on.

"Hey handsome," a male voice said. "I just wanted to see if you'd like to come over and play tonight or— Oh, shit! I forgot! I hope this doesn't reach the wrong ears. Well, if it does, I'm sure you'll straighten it out. I mean, no man should leave his answering machine on with a new beau in the house. Hope I haven't said too much. Call me later. *Ciao!*"

Alfred stood still, his towel hanging from his hand. The books held their breath. In the bathroom the faucet squeaked off. Alfred walked to a chair and dropped down. For a long time, no sound came from anywhere. At last Duane emerged, briskly, drying his hair. He stopped when he saw Alfred.

"What is it? Alfie?"

"You got a message."

Bob could see in Duane's eyes: he knew. But he frowned and said, "What message? Look at you. Did someone die or something?"

"Possibly," said Alfred. "Play it and see."

"Alfie, what are you talking about?"

"Play it, and see."

"Wow! Okay."

Duane stepped over to the machine, pressed the button, and stood with his back to Alfred.

The message played. Before it ended, Duane was already laughing, but not looking at Alfred. "Oh dear!" he sighed, cutting the message off. "You were worried about that?"

Bob saw a flicker of uncertainty in Alfred's eyes. "Tell me why I shouldn't be," he said.

"Oh, he's such a bitch!" Duane laughed. "He does things like that, calling up and saying—"

"He sounded sincere to me."

"Huh?"

"He sounded like he really was saying something he shouldn't. Like he'd forgotten you had a boyfriend here. And maybe the reason he forgot it is that you forgot, too."

"Sweetie," Duane went to him. "What's this all about?"

Alfred recoiled. "Don't tell me I didn't hear that. Don't you tell me I didn't hear what I heard!"

"Alfie! Look— Even if he and I get together sometimes and have a little fun. It doesn't mean anything. He's trash talking. He's got this loopy sense of humor. You can't blame him for that."

Alfred rose. "You're right," he said. "I can't blame him. I can only blame myself if I—"

"What?" said Duane. "I told you he was kidding."

"You've told me a lot," Alfred said, moving away Duane's hand, which was reaching for his penis. "And all you've told me is about

164

him. He's a trash-talker, he's got a sense of humor. You've said nothing about me."

Duane looked nonplused. "What do you want me to say about you?"

"Exactly," Alfred answered, and strode to the bedroom.

Duane followed. "Look, this is the kind of thing gay guys do! Some little thing on the side, some meaningless thing because you've got the urge. I thought we had a fabulous weekend, maybe I was wrong. Look, you're having a very funny reaction to all this, I hope you don't mind me telling you."

Alfred made no reply that the books could hear. Duane turned and came back in their direction: "All right, I am refusing to engage in this. Just because one of my goofy friends left a goofy message there's suddenly this funereal gloom."

Duane erased the message. "I thought we had a wonderful weekend," he called to the bedroom. "I know I did," he added.

A couple of minutes later Alfred appeared, dressed and hair combed. Bob tensed. "Take me," he said suddenly.

Alfred looked darkly at Duane. "I'm going now," he said.

"Take me," said Bob.

"I can't believe this," Duane said, shaking his head and not looking at Alfred.

"Neither can I," said Alfred.

Duane made a bitter little laugh.

"Alfred. Take me. *Now*," Bob said. "I'm more of a friend to you than he is."

Alfred looked at Bob on the table.

"And I'm taking this," he said. In one move he had Bob in hand, and he was gone, down the hall, out the front door, headed for the T. He clutched Bob so hard it hurt.

"It's all right," Bob said. "It sucks, but you're still you. I know. I've been all over the place and had all kinds of things torn apart, some very suddenly. You were there, at the conference, but you didn't see, you didn't know. But in spite of it all I had myself, and you've got yourself, Alfred. And you've got me. We've got each other. And believe me, you did the right thing. You'll never know this, but we were all behind you. His books are fed up with him, the philandering and the indecision. It caught up with him, and he deserved it. Isn't it a nice afternoon? Isn't it nice when you get free of things? Next time you'll know. And there will be a next time, and next time will be better."

Alfred rushed down the stairs to the inbound green line. Once on the train he opened Bob and began rereading him from the beginning.

Chapter 15
Home at Last?

By the time Alfred reached New York in the late October wet, he thought he had learned something from Bob that would help him move ahead with his life. Before, he'd breezed through Bob. This time, coming home on Amtrak, light-headed from thinking how life would be without Duane, he nestled deeply into Bob and for the first time understood a part of Harrison Stone's message: whatever the era, people created and looked at erotica in an attempt to find missing parts of themselves, or to hang on to parts they were terrified to lose. Each era, Stone explained in a chapter called "Aesthetic/Anaesthetic," got the pornography it sought, images that conformed to the ideals of the era, while being transgressive enough to take the observer outside himself. In the case of gay pornography, Stone explained, the models transgressed on behalf of the readers, and also played the roles of ideal mates—muscular, endowed, never effeminate, though they might be boyishly pretty or "innocent." Reading this, Alfred felt a peculiar sense of validation and of being loved and taken care of by the book he held. Stone, through Bob, was telling him he'd been right to break up with Duane.

Alfred remembered his shock at seeing shelves of pornographic DVDs in Duane's bedroom. He'd told himself that most gay men went for this in some form, and that to find a boyfriend utterly uninterested in porn would be impossible, maybe not even desirable. And yet he'd wondered about the glazed look in Duane's eyes when they made love. In order for Duane to reach an orgasm, he needed to be somewhere else. Alfred then turned his questioning on himself. Hadn't Duane looked to him as though he were some kind of idealized image? Alfred clutched Bob gratefully for opening that door for him, helping him realize that he had gone down the wrong path after a boyfriend. *A boyfriend in another city.* He remembered what Stone had said about the "necessarily unbridgeable distance" between viewer and object.

By the time Alfred climbed the steps to his apartment, he was no longer blaming Duane. He was blaming himself—but lightly, taking responsibility in a way that made him feel his rightness and readiness for someone who would love him for who he was. Someone else, or some*thing* else, like a book, could shine a blazing light, but with no pain from the glare, and you saw yourself, more imperfect than ever, surrounded by a brilliant halo.

Ron wasn't there, so Alfred had a lonely homecoming. Bob had a more raucous reception. Alfred tossed him on the table with Angela; the two greeted each joyfully and Angela cried. Bob was happy to see Jerry, too, and even Luke. By now Bob realized it was useless to compete with Luke and his sexy jacket, and Bob noticed something subdued about Luke. He also noticed how in love Jerry and Luke were, which made him rethink his view of Luke.

And then Moishe was lying there, whom Bob had not expected to see. The few words exchanged between them stuck to the subject of how Moishe had come back, and even these words were lost in the mêlée of greetings and inquiries with the other books. But Bob could not ignore Moishe's presence. He tried, wrapping himself up in conversation with Angela, and inquiring in detail about Jerry's and Luke's relationship. Every word Jerry said (he talked more than Luke) reminded Bob that he had a relationship of his own to sort out with Moishe, there beside him.

No one seemed anxious to talk about Luke, least of all Luke himself. That first night Angela would only whisper, "He's been through some difficult times, poor lad." After that, Bob settled down to sleep, trying to ignore Moishe, only to discover that Moishe had gone to sleep even earlier. Bob was still awake when Ron came in. Ron looked down at Alfred's overnight bag, sitting by the entrance to the living room. In one hand Ron carried a plastic bag with a bookstore logo on it. (It looked like a fat paperback. Bob shuddered at the thought that it might be another Tom Clancy book.) Ron went into his bedroom.

The next morning all the books were caught up in the conversation between Alfred and Ron.

"How did it go?" Ron asked, trying not too show too much interest.

For a moment Alfred didn't answer. Ron, though turned to the refrigerator, continued to emit curious vibes. "It went," Alfred said with a sigh, "and then it didn't went. It stopped wenting."

"What do you mean?" Ron tried to keep his voice casual and uninvested.

"I mean it's not going anymore," Alfred said. He looked straight at Ron, gave him a what-else-can-I-say? shrug, and went about preparing his breakfast.

"Oh. Jeez. I'm sorry," Ron said.

Alfred gave another shrug, not looking at Ron.

"I mean, should I be sorry?" Ron continued. "I guess I should. I'm sorry, look—"

"Naw, it's okay," Alfred said. "It was for the best and all that. I was reading the Harrison Stone book on the train. My big liberating gesture was to take it back. So I started to reread it and it really says a lot about looking for the completion of yourself in some kind of iconic thing. He says at the end that, in writing the book, he recovered from being hooked on erotic images. Anyway, Duane was just that: iconic. To me. Too handsome, too unavailable. So you don't have to be too sorry. I learned something about myself. I'm alone again. Feeling a little desperate at the moment, but look, I've got to eat and get going. I'll see you tonight."

Ron went about preparing his own breakfast. After the two men left the apartment, Bob cast a sidelong glance at Moishe. Moishe pretended to be asleep. Finally, Bob said, "Wake up, sleepy head!"

"*Hmmm?*" said Moishe. "Just daydreaming."

"Would you mind if we talked about us?" Bob asked

"All right," Moishe said.

"I just feel unresolved," Bob explained.

"About?"

"About how you feel about me. Tell me again, how did you get back here?"

"Thrown out," Moishe said.

"Thrown out?"

"By her. The woman. You met her."

"But not really thrown out. You're here—"

"Thrown out, yes," Moishe said. He explained how Tovah had sent him back to Ron, bitterly describing the photocopying ordeal.

"So she turned you into a gift," Bob said.

Moishe looked at him blankly.

"I've been one, I should know," said Bob. "It's an honor. In my case things didn't work out; being taken back turned out to be even better. But Tovah wasn't throwing you out. She was giving you up, you, whom she loved, because she knew you'd make someone else even happier."

"Well, I don't know about that," Moishe muttered.

"Well, I do," Bob said. "You're here under a very special set of circumstances. A state of grace. That's greater than any academic work you could be doing. Certainly better than sitting on a shelf."

Moishe seemed not to know what to say. Bob almost thought he'd spoiled some cherished thought Moishe had about his fate. "What about us? I mean, is there any more us?" Bob asked.

Moishe couldn't think which way to go. He had not thought of himself as attached to Bob anymore, until Bob made that observation about his status as a gift. That was beautiful. That was Bob. That was the way Moishe would liked to have thought about the whole incident, if only it had not happened to him.

"Of course," Moishe said, "if you want."

Inside his pages, Bob's heart leapt, but he was careful not to show too much reaction on his cover. He waited to hear more from Moishe.

"I just have to adjust," Moishe shrugged. "I thought my life would be one thing. I had settled into it. Now I'm here. I don't have anything to do anymore."

"Maybe you don't have to do anything," Bob suggested.

Moishe looked at him sharply. "You don't understand," he said. "Work—to know you're useful, doing, moving toward something, busy, busy creating—"

"What if you just sat still," Bob asked, "and enjoyed being a gift? To Ron. To me. What if for a while you didn't stake yourself on doing, doing, doing?"

"And do what?" Moishe demanded.

"Nothing. Or whatever you like. Maybe you've been given a gift, too."

"All the doing didn't provide for me in the end," Moishe muttered.

"So you've been delivered. You're right where you're supposed to be."

Moishe wouldn't completely admit it. But he did allow Bob to get closer. Bob knew better than to say anything more for the moment. He let Moishe think about what he had said. And Moishe would see Jerry and Luke and their togetherness. It would be only a matter of time...

Early that evening the books noticed Ron making an elaborate dinner. He was using Fleur, a new vegetarian cookbook. (Often they heard Fleur sighing to Ina, an older cookbook, "I know how conflicted you must be. You have the word 'joy' in your title, but you can't experience joy, knowing that you're contributing to the suffering of animals.")

Ron set the table for two. "Is there a new fellow we don't know about?" Angela asked. "There hasn't been one in a while," said Jerry.

"But it doesn't look romantic," said Luke. "No candles. Just a normal dinner for two, as though—"

Angela and Luke and Jerry all looked at one another. "Alfred!" they all said together.

"Oh, this should be quite interesting!" Angela said.

When Alfred came home, exhausted, clothes wilted, he looked at the table, frowned, and asked Ron what was up. Ron said, "Just thought I'd cook for us. I knew you'd have a rough day. Relax. It'll be ready in a second."

"Smells great!" Alfred said, and dropped into a dining room chair.

Ron had gone to some lengths. There were homemade ices and cookies for dessert. At the end of the meal, Ron suggested Alfred take a bath while he cleaned up. Alfred gratefully complied.

"He just wants someone to take care of," Jerry observed, as Ron loaded the dishwasher and the shower came on.

"He wants more than that tonight," said Luke. "Besides, even if it is just someone to take care of, what's wrong with that?"

The shower went off. The whir of the dishwasher replaced it. Ron put the leftovers away and turned out the kitchen lights, all but the one under the stove hood. In the half-light he sponged the counter. Alfred came from the bathroom, toweling his hair. He came to the kitchen door.

"This has been so great," he said.

Ron smiled and went on with his chores.

"I feel so taken care of," Alfred said.

Ron sponged the counter. Alfred dried himself and watched Ron. Finally he said, "You want to watch some TV or anything?"

"Sure."

By the time Ron came out of the kitchen, Alfred sat with his feet up, dressed in boxer briefs and a white T-shirt. Ron sat next to him. Alfred channel surfed. "Feel like anything in particular?" he asked.

Ron shook his head. Bob and Angela and Jerry and Luke and Marc and even Moishe all exchanged glances. Ron rose. "Excuse me," he mumbled, and went to his room. Alfred watched him go, then went back switching channels.

Ron reappeared in an undershirt and pajama bottoms. His feet were bare. Without looking at Alfred he sat down, crossed his legs up on a hassock, folded his arms, and watched the changing channels. Alfred settled on a program. Together, they watched in silence. Alfred glanced over at Ron. The books knew this look. Alfred wanted his fuck buddy back. Ron looked at Alfred. But he didn't unfold his arms.

"Wanna have some fun later?" Alfred asked.

Ron shook his head.

"No? Aw, come on, some informal you-know-what. For the hell of it. "

"No," Ron said.

"A wank!" Alfred said, becoming irritated.

"No!"

Alfred stared.

"If you want to make love to me," Ron said, "then make love to me, and we do it in bed and we stay together the whole night."

Alfred looked incredulous.

"I'm in love with you," Ron said. "I finally figured that out. Well, finally let myself realize it and say it. No more wanks. It's love or nothing now. And I hope it's love and I hope it's you. But no quickies. We have to try and make something together. Or I can just move out."

The two stared at one another for several seconds. Slowly, but decisively, Alfred leaned over and gave Ron a gentle, lingering kiss.

The books cheered.

"Come make love to me?" Alfred said, and turned off the TV.

"I say!" said Angela.

"I will," said Ron, and the books cheered some more. Bob even had to wipe away a tear. He glanced at Moishe, who was doing his best to control his response, looking wistful and deeply involved in what was going on.

Alfred and Ron gently slid into each other's arms, touching as though each of them was delicate and breakable, as though each might lose the other if he laid a hand too heavily. They stayed in that awkward, careful clinch for several minutes before Alfred said, "I didn't know."

"Maybe I didn't know," Ron said.

"If I'd just looked—" Alfred began.

"If we all looked a little closer," Ron concluded, quietly.

Alfred kissed the top of Ron's head. "What do we do now?"

"Nothing," Ron said.

"What do you mean?"

"We got this far," Ron explained. "Everything else takes care of itself later. This is the reward. I don't want to get up. I might spoil it."

Alfred shook his head. "No, you won't," he said. "But I don't think you should get up yet."

No one, book or man, said a word. After several more minutes, Alfred and Ron retired to Alfred's room. The books could not hear a sound from behind the closed door.

📖

The next afternoon, Ron presented Alfred with the small bookstore bag from the day before.

"What's this?" Alfred said. He pulled out a brand new paperback copy of *Vanity Fair*.

"You said once that you'd always wanted to read it, that you missed classics, so I got it for you," Ron said. "Well, well," said Angela. "English literature. I do approve."

Alfred hugged Ron and thanked him. "This is wonderful," he said, holding the new book in both his hands. "You know, Duane had all those books but he didn't really care. Oops, sorry!"

"That's okay," Ron said quietly. "That's over."

"Yes," Alfred agreed. "That's over."

He placed the copy of *Vanity Fair* on the table top, right next to Angela.

"Hello," Angela said crisply.

"How do?" said the Thackeray book, in a deep voice. He introduced himself as Thomas.

"Pleased to meet you, Thomas," Angela said. Jerry, Luke, Bob, Marc, and Moishe exchanged glances, and Jerry looked amused. Thomas and Angela continued to talk, and found they had many things in common, in addition to being paperback editions of

English classics. They had temperaments that naturally fit, and they talked long into the night.

"Well, it looks as though Angela's had a happy accident," Bob said to Moishe, after everyone else had fallen asleep.

"So has this fellow Tom," Moishe said.

"Of course," Bob added, thinking suddenly of Sunny, "there are no accidents."

"No," Moishe said, "I suppose there aren't." That was all he said that night.

Bob had been back in Alfred's and Ron's apartment for several days now, but he and Luke had not reconciled. Bob noticed Luke's quietness and reduced circumstances, but he remembered how snooty Luke had been. Angela had suggested that Bob be sympathetic and understanding, but decency, she said, prevented her from telling him why. "Other than that he's a fellow book, subjected to all the same trials and indignities as you!" she'd declared hotly. Bob decided to accept this. Angela rarely lashed out, so her meaning had to be serious—and he tried to be nice to Luke.

But he still felt inferior. Luke had the sexy cover (slightly torn now, but in that way even more rakish) and had plenty of hot pictures. Bob's nudes were muscular, even handsome after a style, but silly-looking in ducktails and posing straps. Bob thought he was too text-heavy. No matter how reduced his circumstances, Luke had the sleek, sexy, worldly look. And he had Jerry's love.

Strange, Bob thought, because Jerry, in spite of the liberal slant of his text, was kind of square. And the smoke smell. Bob realized, though, that he loved Moishe, who was not sleek like Luke. Moishe was skinny and temperamental. *What dictated love? How and when and why did it happen?* Could it really happen again between him and Moishe?

📖

"Look what's on the Queer Cable channel!" Ron called to Alfred. Alfred was preparing dinner; the romance between the roommates was going well, as far as Bob could see. Bob had had several long conversations with Moishe, mostly about their adventures and how they'd felt about them. Bob felt warm and close to Moishe, and he suspected Moishe felt the same about him. Moishe had not said anything definite, and Bob had not asked. But they seemed to move closer and closer to one another, just like their old Gay Diversions days. Thomas and Angela, now quite close, urged Bob on, but Bob had yet to put it straight to Moishe.

"What?" asked Alfred.

"Our friend Harrison Stone."

"Let's watch."

The interview came on at half-past eleven. Alfred switched over from his *Golden Girls* rerun to the gay channel. The TV shone in the book-lined room, along with a small lamp over Bob, Moishe, Angela, and Thomas. Jerry and Luke reclined on their shelf, and Luke looked nervous. "I remember what he said about me before," he told the others. "I don't know if I want to hear this."

"You don't have to watch if you don't want to," Jerry said. "But you could at least give him a chance. Maybe he's changed his mind."

"I doubt it!" Luke muttered, but he agreed to watch.

The interviewer asked right off the bat: "Harrison, you've been quoted as condemning the manner in which you were forced to publish your second book." Alfred's books held their breath. "You've said the publishers cheapened it."

"Yes," said Stone. "I said that."

"Do you still feel that way?"

"I no longer feel that way," said Stone.

"Really?" said the interviewer. "Why?"

"I think that my original vision for that book was too staid, too scholarly," Stone began. "I wanted to withhold erotic pleasure from readers, because I myself resented the good looks of those porn stars, how free they were, how admired and so forth. Now I can't condone that in myself. I also can't condone the publisher changing my vision. But the upshot of the publisher's decision to add explicit pictures and trim down my text has been that the book is more accessible. I look it over now and I see that the message remains, how we escaped from our problems through those fantasies, how we avoided AIDS and loneliness and compulsion. There are some beautiful boys in those pages. Some who have died. Beauty can be a nice and instructive and satisfying thing. So long as you're not longing to *be* one of those boys, as I was. I remember how excitedly I ran to the bookstore where I found most of those images." Bob and Moishe smiled at one another.

"If you can take something from the image of a boy, or use something in it to ignite a special quality in yourself, and if you can use that to do something positive for yourself or others, then why not spread it all out there? Dicks, asses, balls, tits, everything. That's the spirit in which people should read my second book. Read that way, it's a wonderful book."

Everyone looked at Luke. He blushed.

"But the first book is really more to your taste, right?" Stone's interviewer asked.

"The first one speaks about an entirely different era, and when I wrote it I was a different person. I am happy with both my books. I have to see the good in me that produced the good in them. The publishers also made decisions about the first one that I didn't agree with at the time."

Bob started. He hadn't known this.

"But with time I either changed my mind and realized the publishers were right, or I let go. Books are like kids. You have to love them in spite of and then love them because of."

Bob looked up at Luke, and found Luke looking back at him.

"So I'd recommend both books to everyone!" Stone said, looking straight into the camera.

Bob and Luke smiled at one another. Then Bob became aware of Moishe, pressing against him. Moishe had come out of himself enough to love this moment for its reflection on another and to love the other on whom Stone's light shone. Bob was touched. He had doubted that Moishe had this in him. But just as it does whenever anyone surprises us, love leapt up in Bob, and he pressed back. And Moishe did not let up.

When the Stone interview ended, there were congratulations all around for Bob and Luke. Bob realized he felt happier for Luke than for himself. That pleased him. Ron and Alfred retired Ron's room. Bob decided he felt bold and confident enough to speak to Moishe about their possible future together.

"It was a nice program, wasn't it?" Bob said.

"Beautiful," said Moishe.

"'Beautiful?'" Bob asked. He rarely heard such effusions from Moishe.

"It had so much to say," Moishe said. "I guess... I suppose I learned a few things."

Bob couldn't help saying, "Gee, don't commit yourself!" which Moishe greeted with a rueful chuckle.

"Things change so much," Moishe said after a moment. "Things you counted on. Or disappointments. Like your man, Stone. He thought he'd resent his publisher forever, but he rethought things. The way you rethought some things for me." It came on Moishe full force, the thought he had had that he was a helper and Bob was not. He swore he would never tell Bob or anyone about it. Instead he mumbled, "You said I was a gift."

"I meant that in more than one way."

"I'm still not convinced that being a 'gift' to Ron makes up for all I lost. But, just the fact that you want it to be true for me."

"But did you hear what I said? You're a gift in more than one way."

"Why, though? I let you down. How could I be a gift now?"

"Because I rethink things myself. Whatever happens, just having you close these past few days, if that's all the gift I get, it's enough."

And so Bob, who'd thought his question to Moishe would be about the future, had ended up making a statement about the present.

"We hope it's more than just here and now," Moishe mumbled.

"We don't know," Bob said. "That would be nice. But right now, we have this, and this is awfully nice."

Moishe pressed against him, and his voice broke when he said, "Yes, yes it is. Thank you, *bubbeleh.*"

For a moment there was no sound in the darkened living room. And then just behind him Bob heard Angela's crisp whisper, "Good show, lads! Good show!"

Isaac arrived home late to his small apartment in Hoboken. That evening, his friend Chaim had given him a gift of a small book of gay love poems. He had flipped through Neil on the PATH train, then put him in his satchel. Now, entering Isaac's darkened apartment, Neil's heart quickened with anticipation. Life among a new set of books! Who would they be? What would they be like? Would one of them be interesting, in *that way?* Neil wished it were daylight so he could see his new comrades clearly. Isaac unpacked him. Neil heard murmurs of interest from other books, but he could not see them well.

There were hundreds of bindings arrayed in the stripes of moonlight criss-crossing the little living room. Neil was suddenly afraid. He remembered the hostilities among those in Owen's book collection. *Would that happen here?* He heard whispers:

"Who is it?"

"Looks skinny."

"Some kind of novelty thing?"

Neil had never been referred to this way before, and it made him sad and resentful. Maybe he'd just keep to himself, or hope to end up on Isaac's night table, like many gift or novelty books.

Isaac placed him on a shelf with a number of towering, thick volumes he could not identify. "You a gift book?" one asked.

"I suppose," Neil said. "I was given as a—"

"What's in you? I can't read in this light."

"Er... love poems," Neil said. He decided to leave out the gay part. Wisely, he thought, as he could now make out, in the dim light, that this was a biography of a business magnate, who appeared in a suit and tie on the cover. Such a book was not likely to be sympathetic.

"Y'mean like Shakespeare?"

"Yes, a couple by Shakespeare," Neil said.

"Yeah, but what's your theme?" the other book demanded. "Gotta have a theme to succeed in this world! Some way to measure results!"

"It's... gay love poems," Neil finally confessed.

"What's that?"

"Gay love poems," Neil said, louder.

"Gay love poems?" said the other. "Jeez, what kind of readership you get for that? Not much, I guess. Terrible cost ratio."

"Well, Isaac seems—"

"But you said you were a gift. Kinda book everyone gives, but no one reads, ha-ha! But that can work. It's all marketing."

Neil felt wounded and was trying to think of a reply—even though this was the kind of book no one could ever truly reply to—when suddenly another voice spoke up: "I am wrothe wyth ye!" it cried at the business book. "For thys is my fealow, veryly!" Neil gasped and looked around. There on his other side was a familiar and handsome orange cover, with two knights riding side by side.

"You!" Neil said.

"Gretyngs!" cried the edition of Malory. "Lat me helpe ye now, whatsomever com of hit, that youre herte shal be pleasyd!"

"That my heart shall be pleased?" Neil said.

"Ay!" said the orange-covered book.

"But why?" Neil said, with a little laugh.

"For love of ye!" said the orange-covered book.

Neil squinted in the moonlight and saw the amorous way in which this book was looking at him. "You're kidding!" Neil said. "Malory? *Gay?*"

"Ay!" the book said, and it leaned a tad closer.

"Wow!" Neil said. The business book had backed off now. "What do you know about that?"

Neil thought back to when he met the Malory book. On that table in the Armory were three musketeers, who hoped to be sold together. It never happened. Neil had hoped to be reunited with Jerry. That didn't happen, either, nor had things worked out with Marc. And now, this.

Bob and Angela would say he should take this. And Jerry, wherever he was, would say so, too. Jerry knew you had to take love where you found it. That's what the two of them had done, once upon a time, so long ago and so far from here. Neil hoped Jerry, if he was alive, had found love, too. He thought he would weep if he thought of that one more second. Instead, he turned his gaze up at his tall, orange friend, gazing so warmly, so hopefully down at him.

He thought maybe he had found home, at least for now. Rough but gentle, strange but familiar, as it always was.

Acknowledgements

My parents read me and told me a great many stories, about everything from Mowgli to talking animals to the minutemen who defended my mother's hometown of Concord, Mass. At the Loomis Chaffee School, Rennie McQuilken, Brian Davidson, and Sam Pierson all encouraged me greatly.

In the years leading up to *Bob*, I had the support of several writing groups to which I belonged. Three Hots and a Cot introduced me to many prominent gay writers, gave me reading opportunities, and taught me about the business of writing: thank you Achim Nowak, Mike Thomas, Rebecca Shannonhouse, Ron Caldwell, Tim Driscoll, and Janet Crawford. Karin Cook, the late Kenneth King, Jenifer Levin, Darcey Steinke, Dale Peck, and Jill Ciment were all fine teachers. When their workshops broke up I continued working with my fellow students, receiving supportive advice from Donna Allegra, Eileen O'Toole, Joe Stamps, Laurie Piette, Tom Weber, and again, Janet Crawford. Benjamin Birdie, Sarah Durham and David Corrado were great comrades and readers. *Bob* was part of my contribution to a summer project I hatched with grad school friends called "101 Stories in 101 Days." A special thanks to Ellen for being *Bob*'s first huge fan.

His second huge fan was Rogério M. Pinto, Ph.D., who is always and forever my fan, too, no matter what. *Te amo, Doce.* Thank you for being a friend.

Mary Ed Porter always said I should be a writer, and she has occupied the front row at many a reading, as have Rosemarie Sciarrone, Blossom Milyoner, Marlene Fortes, Deborah Unger, and many of those listed above. I thank them all, and I thank Joey Brenneman and Stacey Linden of *Above the Bridge* for giving *Bob* its first reading.

Jim Currier of Chelsea Station first read *Bob* when I submitted it to an LGBT writing contest for which he was a judge. The book did not win, but Jim told me how much he liked it and said that, if he were a publisher he would publish it. Now he is, and now he has, and he has been the most supportive, lowest-drama publisher I could imagine.

Andrew Farber guided the final dotting of i's and crossing of t's, Eva Mueller made me look much better than I really do, and Brandon Epting is just generally great about everything and so must be mentioned.

About the Author

DAVID PRATT has published short fiction in *Christopher Street, The James White Review, Blithe House Quarterly, Harrington Gay Men's Fiction Quarterly, Velvet Mafia, Lodestar Quarterly,* and other periodicals, and in the anthologies *Men Seeking Men, His[3]* and *Fresh Men 2.* He has directed and performed his own work for the theater, including appearances in New York City at the Cornelia Street Café, Dixon Place, HERE Arts Center, the Flea Theater, Theater of the Elephant, and the Eighth Annual New York International Fringe Festival. He has collaborated frequently with Rogério M. Pinto, and he was the first director of several plays by the Canadian playwright John Mighton. David holds an MFA in Creative Writing from the New School. *Bob the Book* is the second novel he has written, and it is the first to be published. He is currently at work on the book of a new musical.

Lightning Source UK Ltd.
Milton Keynes UK
01 February 2011

166719UK00002B/85/P